Thunderbird
Cryptid Ops Book 1
By Jo Carey

COPYRIGHT

Original cover art by Catherine Archer-Wills
www.facebook.com/carcherwillsdesign

ISBN-13: 978-1-944946-45-6
ISBN-10: 1944946454

CHAPTER ONE

It was one hundred and five degrees in the shade. Well, it might be if any shade could be found in the Chihuahuan Desert of southern New Mexico. Cassie loved the desert heat and always took the necessary precautions—lots of sunscreen, hat, plenty of water. The desert exposed the geology that made rock collecting here so much fun. Layers of Earth's geological history were visible in the multi-hued rocks.

She had parked her ATV in the shade of some mesquite bushes and hiked to the rock face she wanted to check out. One of the best parts of being in the desert on a hot day was the solitude. Not that this area was ever crawling with people, but when the temperature soared, the excessive heat kept all but the hardiest, or some might say craziest, people indoors. Cassie loved being out in the desert alone. She found the solitude peaceful. She understood the risks and thought she was well prepared for any emergency.

The desert was Cassie's happy place. With chisel in hand working an interesting mineral seam, she was having a terrific day. Rock hunting for Cassie was more about the hunt and less about finding a big score. It was mindless work. While you were pounding hammer on chisel, your mind was free to concentrate on other things.

Tony would usually have been with her, but he had to work. To be honest, right now, Cassie preferred to be alone. Tony was her college sweetheart and first serious relationship, but she felt she'd matured and changed while Tony had stayed the same. These days the two of them spent a lot of time arguing. Cassie wasn't a confrontational person. They both realized that something needed to change, yet neither wanted to be the one

1

to end things. Sometimes you just got comfortable with the status quo and didn't want to rock the boat.

When Cassie stood to stretch out her back muscles and get a drink water, she turned in a slow circle soaking in the desert scenery. She stopped mid-turn, thinking she had seen something move off to the west near a line of red rocks. She stood still, watching, but with the glare of the sun, she couldn't be sure if there was something there or not. Though she was comfortable in the desert alone, she knew you had to be cautious. The remote areas of the Desert Southwest were sometimes used by drug cartels to move their cargo into the country which added an element of danger that Cassie took care to avoid.

After standing still for a few minutes and seeing no further sign of movement, she returned to her mineral seam. She planned to spend another hour or two breaking rocks before heading back to town. Chiseling rock is intense work. Cassie was on her knees, shoulder bent low working with chisel and sledge hammer to loosen pieces from the fluorite vein in the rock face. She would examine the small stones that now littered the ground in front of the rocks and maybe take home a few nice samples for her collection.

Unlike a forest, the desert is a quiet place, but Cassie's hammer and chisel were making so much noise she didn't hear the men approaching until a shadow crept over the rock face she was working. Cassie knew she was in trouble.

With a firm grasp on her tools, she stood up and turned to see three men staring at her. They wore stained shirts and dirty ripped jeans. She could see that at least one of them was carrying a gun. Cassie had her back to the rock outcropping and faced them. She started edging along the rocks preparing to make a run for it if the opportunity arose. "How are you guys doing today? Are you enjoying the desert?" she asked, trying to sound casual.

"Doin' OK, but our Jeep broke down. We thought we were headed to the road, but I guess we're lost," said the tallest one. "Do you have a car nearby? Can you give us a lift back to town?"

"I'm sorry. I hiked in this morning from the campground five miles west of here. I'll be happy to point you in the right direction or draw you a map. I have an extra bottle of water if that helps."

"Water would be great. You should lead us out so we don't get lost again," said the tall guy.

"Sorry, guys. I've got a couple more hours of work to do here before I'm ready to head back. You'll be fine. It's an easy hike once you're pointed in the right direction."

The man nearest to the end of the rocks that Cassie had been moving along stepped over and placed his hand on the stones to block her escape route. "Well sure, I guess I can do that if you can't manage on your own. Just give me a couple minutes to gather up my tools and samples," Cassie told them. She bent down and started putting items back into her pack. They kept a close eye on her. She handed them a bottle of water hoping to distract them while she hid the chisel in the pocket of her cargo pants. She wished she had a gun, but the chisel would have to do. When she had packed up her gear, she led the group off into the desert heading east.

CHAPTER TWO

Cassie weighed her options, as they walked. If she led them west, they would reach the road or her ATV in a couple of hours, but Cassie didn't think they wanted to get to the road and was afraid that any sign of people would cause them to react in a way that would be bad for her and maybe others too. She knew the area well and hoped she'd be able to tire them out by leading them into harsher terrain. It was a crap shoot at best. She decided she'd take her chances with the desert. She'd use all her desert knowledge to escape.

She led them to a hilly area she was familiar with where there was a mine. She had explored the mine tunnels extensively. The BLM rangers had some emergency supplies stashed there, and Cassie hoped she could lose her captors long enough to escape into the tunnels and hide. She could hold up there until the men grew bored and moved on. She was confident in her plan and hoped the trek through the extreme desert heat might take some of the fight out of her captors.

The group trekked on in silence, stopping every few minutes to drink water or wipe the sweat from their eyes. Leading the way, Cassie was able to formulate her plan and review it in detail as she led them deeper into the desert. The further they went, the more convinced she was that the men intended to do her harm. That realization gave her the conviction she needed to do whatever was necessary to escape. The first step in her plan was to find a way to reduce the number of her captors. Three-to-one wasn't good odds unless she was armed. A world-ranked competitor in rifle competitions, Cassie was confident in her shooting skills. If she was armed and got a chance to fire her weapon, she knew she could disable her captors, but she didn't normally take a gun when she went out hiking. After today, that was something she'd change.

Approaching a line of small, scree-covered hills, Cassie turned to the men, "Sorry guys, it's a little rough cutting through here, but it will shorten our walk." The men said nothing but continued to plod along behind her in silence. Earlier in the year, Cassie had helped her BLM co-workers relocate some diamondback rattlesnakes from a popular hiking trail to this ridge. She had checked on the snakes and knew where they'd made their new home. She planned to lead the men on a path that would take them right by the snakes' den. With any luck one of the men might be careless and end up a snakebite victim. She intended to do everything in her power to make sure that happened.

A few minutes later, Cassie led the men to an outcropping and used her hands to scramble up the rock face. She saw one of the snakes. She chose her handholds with care to avoid it, but wanted to ensure that one of the men wasn't so lucky. Just above the level of the snakes' hiding place, she knocked some rock loose so that it tumbled down the hillside alerting the snake that something had strayed into its domain. She looked back over her shoulder and suggested to the man behind her that he might want to choose a path a bit to the left of her route to avoid the loose rock. It worked like a charm. The man placed his hand down right in front of the snake. The rattler struck immediately. The man screamed and pulled back his hand, a small trickle of blood flowed from the bite.

Cassie hoped the snake had helped her out by injecting its full load of venom. The bite of the western diamondback is poisonous but seldom deadly, if the victim reaches medical treatment within thirty minutes of receiving the bite. The men rushed to their fallen comrade and carried him away from the snake. Cassie wondered why they didn't shoot the snake. She had only seen the one gun. This could be an indication that they had limited ammunition or didn't want to risk attracting unwanted attention by firing a weapon.

"Oh crap! If we don't get him to the hospital in the next thirty minutes, he's going to die," explained Cassie. She noticed the other two men exchange a look, but they remained silent. "Our best chance to save him is to get help as soon as possible. We'll never make it to the road in time. I'm more used to the desert than you guys. I'll run ahead and get to a phone."

Cassie wasn't sure what she expected to happen, but she was shocked when the big guy said with a shrug, "Leave him here. We'll bring back help."

Cassie pleaded, explaining that by the time they reached civilization, help wouldn't be able to get to the man in time, but the men ignored her. Cassie realized that, although this wasn't the reaction she'd expected, it did accomplish her goal of limiting the number of men she had to deal with. The big guy bent and whispered something to his fallen comrade, and motioned to Cassie, "Move out."

She started working out the next step in her plan as she plodded along. *One down, two to go*, she thought. They were making good progress, but the route she was following only led further into the desert. Cassie's cell phone rang. She answered it automatically, but the big guy stepped up and jerked it from her before she could say anything. He grasped one of her arms while he turned the phone off and put it in his shirt pocket. He squeezed her upper arm so hard it hurt like hell, but she wouldn't give him the satisfaction of screaming. He let go of her arm and shoved her forward.

"What the hell? I could have had them send help for your friend," she said.

It was Tony's ringtone. She knew he would keep trying to reach her. Cell phone coverage in the desert was strange. Sometimes you could walk just a few yards off the main road and not have a signal, and other times you'd be in the middle of nowhere and your phone would ring. It gave her hope to know that if she was unable to answer his call, Tony would eventually realize something was wrong and start searching for her. She hoped he still cared enough.

After hiking a few more minutes, they stopped for a water break. The tall man was getting a little too friendly with Cassie, touching her hair and looking at her in a way that made her skin crawl. She could brush-off his advances for now, but knew that she needed to escape soon. Thankfully, they were nearing the old mine. She was preparing for the next phase of her plan. Cassie led them down into a steep-sided arroyo. The ocotillo plants had long sharp thorns, but Cassie moved through them with practiced ease. The two men behind her started swearing each time the bushes scratched them. They were slowing down considerably, which is what she hoped would happen.

There was a sharp bend in the arroyo coming up, and that's where Cassie planned to make a break for it. She sped up as much as possible without being obvious which allowed her to get ahead of her captors by nearly fifty yards. As soon as she turned the corner, she took off running. She crouched low to take advantage of the sparse cover. It took a few seconds before she heard the big guy yell, "Get her!"

She didn't look back. She kept going and jumped down into another arroyo where she would be out of sight of the two men for a few seconds. She ran close to the side, hoping her footprints would be less obvious. Cassie ducked behind the rock pile that hid the old mine entrance and ran into the tunnels.

X X X

Just a few yards in from the entrance, daylight was extinguished completely, but Cassie knew these tunnels well and continued past the first split before she had to have light to move safely. She leaned back against the smooth rock wall and caught her breath. She fished around in the pockets of her cargo pants and found her key chain with the small flashlight attached. She rested for a few minutes listening for any sound of her pursuers. The silence was broken only by the drumbeat of her heart in her ears.

After several minutes of silence with no sign of her pursuers, Cassie turned on the light and moved deeper into the mine as quickly and quietly as a lizard. The mine was on BLM land in a barren part of the desert. The rangers used the tunnels to store survival supplies deep enough in the mine so as not to be found by a casual explorer, but they all knew how to locate the stash, if it was needed.

Unlike caves or mines in many other parts of the country, mine tunnels in New Mexico are usually very dry, so the supplies kept well throughout the year. The mine was located in the middle of an area that Cassie often visited alone, and though comfortable in the desert, she always felt better knowing the supplies were there. Flash floods, though infrequent, posed a real threat when hiking in the arroyos. Lightning was a major concern during the summer monsoon season. The mine provided extra supplies, shelter from the elements and, she hoped, an obvious spot to locate her, if she required rescue.

She stopped every few minutes and listened for any sign of her captors, but she heard nothing. Cassie was relieved, but didn't believe they would give up so easily. She had no idea what they intended to do with her, but the way they acted when her phone rang made it clear that they had some interest in her that went beyond helping them get back to civilization. She kept her guard up and kept moving. When she reached the stash of supplies, she gulped downed a bottle of water and ate a granola bar to give her some energy. She sat down on a bin to decide what to do next.

The mine was about three miles from where she left her ATV and the desert in between would provide little cover. Without her cell phone, she had no way to call for help. She would have to get herself out of this mess. *We really should add a burner phone to the supply stash,* she thought to herself.

Cassie planned to stay put until sundown when the weather would be cooler and the dark would provide cover for her escape, if the men were still in the area. She decided to set up a couple of early warning signals along the tunnel leading to the supply area. She piled rocks across the tunnel every few feet. She hoped anyone walking down the tunnel would knock over the piles which would make noise and alert her. If that happened, she'd continue deeper into the mine and hope she could lose them. The mine had no other exit that she'd ever found. Cassie looked through the supply bin hoping she might find something to use as a weapon, but she came up empty. She spread out a space blanket behind the pile of supplies and sat down to rest.

She planned to take a circuitous route back to her ATV using whatever sparse cover she could find. Once she reached the vehicle, she'd head back to Rob's. This was the first time

Cassie could ever remember not feeling safe in the desert. She hated it. The tension and exertion of the day took its toll, and she soon fell into a deep sleep.

Cassie screamed when a hard slap to the face woke her. The tall guy and his companion loomed over her. She had no idea how they found her, but it was clear that they weren't happy she'd escaped.

"You thought you could out-smart us," said the tall man, pointing his gun in her direction. "Now, do what I say and cause no more trouble, or I'll make you wish I had killed you sooner."

The men took water and food from the supply stash and sat down to eat, keeping Cassie trapped between them. Once they finished, the shorter man checked his watch. "We must go now to make our handoff," he said. The other man waved Cassie to her feet with the gun and fell in behind her as they moved back up the tunnels and out of the mine. Cassie had to figure out a way to escape once more. She decided to see which way the men headed before deciding on a plan of attack.

X X X

After a few minutes' walk, Cassie realized they were heading toward an old ghost town south of where she had parked the ATV. There were rumors that drug dealers used the old ruins to move product into the US, and she suspected that's what these men were involved in. She needed to escape before they met up with their friends. Cassie visualized the route they would take. She knew they would soon pass by the stone ruins of a rancher's cabin. She'd make her move there.

The desert gods were watching over Cassie. Before reaching the ruins, she stumbled over a large rock in the trail and fell to her knees. The big guy grabbed her by her arms and lifted her back to her feet. As luck would have it, Cassie's fall caused her to hit her knee on the chisel in her cargo pants pocket. It would cause a bruise, but it reminded her that she did have a weapon.

As they continued walking, Cassie eased the chisel from her pocket and gripped it as though it were a lifeline. As they dropped down into an arroyo, Cassie veered to one side causing the man with the gun to trip over a rock and put his hands down to brace his fall. With no hesitation, she turned and thrust the chisel into the back of the man's gun hand with all the force she could muster. As he screamed in pain, she stepped on the top of the chisel with her foot, putting all her weight on it, pinning the man's hand to the ground. In one swift motion, she lunged for the gun, grabbed it from his hand, and shot the other man in the leg. He tumbled over some rocks grasping his thigh as blood spurted from the wound. Cassie had gotten lucky again. She'd hit an artery. If they didn't stop the bleeding soon, the man would bleed out. If they did get the bleeding stopped, he would have difficulty walking. She hoped neither of them would be able to chase her.

CHAPTER THREE

Cassie held on to the gun and ran in the direction of her ATV. For a few minutes, she heard the two men screaming and yelling at each other. Eventually, she had run far enough that the voices faded into the distance.

She still needed to be cautious, but move quickly. Unfortunately, there was little moonlight, and she was less familiar with this area. Cassie stumbled and fell hitting her head on a large rock. She lost consciousness and the gun.

When she came to, her head throbbed. She tried to check her wristwatch, but her vision blurred. When she wiped at her eyes, her hand came away dark with blood. *Damn, I just can't catch a break today*, she thought to herself as she leaned on the rocks to get to a standing position. She got her extra shirt out of her pack and used it to clean the blood from her face and eyes. She could feel the cut on her head, so she balled up the shirt and held it against the wound to stop the bleeding. She looked around for the gun, but didn't see it. Wobbly, but otherwise okay, she started moving slowly toward where she thought she'd left the ATV. She was nauseous and dizzy. She knew those were signs that she probably had a concussion, but as long as she was able to move, she was confident in her ability to survive. She fished out her pocket first-aid kit, took two Tylenol without water, and kept walking.

Cassie watched a lot of survival shows on TV and read many books on the subject. She knew that often the main factor in surviving when stranded in a remote area came down to forcing yourself to keep putting one foot in front of the other. She concentrated on each step, counting them as she went. She lost count several times and started over.

She didn't know how long she'd been walking before she noticed the pre-dawn light beginning to erase the darkness from the edges of the desert. She kept going until she fell to her knees in exhaustion. *Where is the ATV? I should have reached it by now,* Cassie thought. She sat down, leaning her back against a rocky outcropping to rest for a few minutes. It was a mammoth struggle not to give in to the despair that hovered just at the edge of her thoughts. She hoped that daylight would bring some familiar landmark into view so she could get her bearings and not wander aimlessly around the desert.

She dozed off for a bit. When she opened her eyes again, her head still throbbed like the drum line in a marching band, but her vision had cleared. She slowly stood up and pivoted in a full circle, looking for something familiar. She saw rocks, sand, cactus, and creosote bushes. Nothing looked familiar, but then again, it all looked familiar.

A brief pang of panic struck, but it was short lived. She took two more Tylenol from the small first-aid kit and remembered the water bottle in her pants pocket. She tried to save some of the water. Her mouth was so dry she had to pull her tongue loose from the roof of her mouth to drink. It took every ounce of her willpower not to down the water in one gulp. She held the liquid in her mouth as long as she could, letting it sooth her dry mouth before swallowing. After closing her eyes for a few more minutes, her mind started to clear, and she began to formulate a plan. With the sun fully up, she was able to navigate and head due west. West would eventually lead her back to the road, but she hoped she'd find the ATV first.

She braced her hands on the rock wall to help her get to a standing position and test her balance. As she pushed off from the rocks, she noticed something odd in the sand at her feet. She could see several tracks. Each track was huge. The X-shape looked vaguely familiar, but Cassie's head hurt too badly to think about it. Without thinking, she started to follow the tracks. *Wait. What am I doing? I need to get out of here*, she told herself. Maybe she and Tony could come back and photograph the tracks. She could report them to her BLM colleagues. She couldn't think straight. Her head was spinning. Cassie moved off into the barren desert putting one foot in front of the other again.

CHAPTER FOUR

Back in Las Cruces, Tony packed up his gear. He was worried sick about Cassie. He'd been trying to call her every thirty minutes since late yesterday afternoon. He knew she could take care of herself, and cell coverage in the desert could be unreliable, but she would never stay away overnight without letting him know, unless she was in serious trouble. The first time he'd tried to reach her, someone answered, but then the phone went dead.

Tony and Cassie had been together since they met during their junior year at Arizona State. They seemed to be fighting more lately. He sensed they were reaching a decision point in their relationship. Right now, none of that mattered.

Tony spent last night calling all of Cassie's friends and co-workers, but no one had heard anything from her. Ranger Bob told him that Cassie stopped by the office that morning on her way to the Last Hope Mine area.

Late last night, Tony's buddy Rob called asking if everything was alright. Cassie had parked her SUV at his house when she headed off on the ATV. When she didn't return by dark, he got concerned and tried calling her, but she didn't answer. Tony explained the situation and asked for Rob's help. Both Tony and Rob were part of the local search and rescue squad. They agreed that if Cassie wasn't home safe by morning, they'd meet at Rob's house and start searching for her.

X X X

Tony was waiting in Rob's driveway before sunrise.

"How are you holding up?" Rob asked as he raised the garage door.

"As well as I can be at this point. I'm trying to focus on finding her and not think about all the things that could have happened," Tony answered.

"If you want, I'll call the search and rescue squad. They've all worked with Cassie on searches. I know they'd be glad to help," he offered.

"We might need to do that in a few hours, but I'd like to see if we can handle it ourselves first. Let's try to figure out where she was. That will give the search team a place to start," Tony said.

Rob took out a map of the wilderness area, and they discussed their search route. Tony knew where Cassie would have parked the ATV if she went to the Last Hope Mine, so they decided to head there first and see if they could find any clues to what direction she headed from that point. They loaded their gear onto Rob's ATV and headed out, stopping every thirty minutes to drink water and scan the area with binoculars for any sign of Cassie. If there was cell service when they took a break, they called Rob's wife, Sue, to report their location. Rob's experience with Search and Rescue had taught him that the searchers needed to be extra diligent about their own safety. All too often, searchers ended up needing rescue along with the original victim.

They found Cassie's ATV and there was no evidence of any mechanical problem. There were no prints around the vehicle other than Cassie's. Fortunately, there was little wind, so they were able to follow her footprints for a while. When they lost the trail, Tony suggested they continue on to an outcropping where he thought she might have been rock hounding.

They easily found the mineral seam Cassie had been working with her chisel and noticed some partial shoe prints in the same area. They recognized the print of Cassie's hiking boots and could pick out at least three sets of larger prints.

"I don't like the look of this," Tony said. "There are rarely many people out here this time of the year. I hope's she's okay."

"Come on, Tony. Don't let it worry you. It could be anything. Remember, Cassie is one kick-ass chick. She can take care of herself, especially out here. This is her element. I'm sure she's fine."

It was clear that Cassie had been there, but none of her gear was there. Tony didn't know if that was a good or bad sign or if it didn't really matter. He hoped it meant she had some things with her to help her survive whatever was going on.

Tony took a survival whistle out of his pack and blew it several times. They listened but there was no response. After drinking water and eating power bars, they decided to head to the abandoned mine where the BLM rangers stored survival supplies. If something went wrong, that's where Cassie would go, if she could.

CHAPTER FIVE

Cassie kept walking, putting one foot in front of the other. She realized she no longer noticed the pain from the bump on her head. She wondered whether that was a good or bad thing. She had finished the last of her water. With the sun up, she knew she was heading west. She believed she would eventually find a landmark she recognized. She hoped to reach the mine. She'd need the supplies stored there to be able to make it back to her ATV in the heat of the day.

By now, Tony would be somewhere out here searching for her. Even though they were having problems lately, he'd be worried about her. If he had called the BLM office, they would have notified all the rangers on patrol to be looking for her as well. She felt sure she'd soon cross paths with someone who would help. A small dissenting voice added, *or run into more of the people those men were meeting in the desert.* She told that voice to keep its damn opinions to itself.

X X X

On the way to the mine, Tony and Rob found footprints that seemed to be headed in that direction, but then the tracks veered off. They agreed that if they didn't find Cassie at the mine, they'd backtrack and follow the prints. They entered the main tunnel and Rob led the way to the supply cache. The local search and rescue squad used the stash, too. It was obvious that someone had been there recently. They hoped it was Cassie. Several empty water bottles were scattered around the area along with granola wrappers. Tony knew Cassie wouldn't have left the trash in the mine. She would have packed it out. There was a space blanket spread out on the floor.

The mine tunnel was smooth, so there were no footprints to provide any clues to help them identify who had used the supplies. When Tony picked up the blanket to replace it in the bin, a yellow sticky note fell off and floated to the ground. He picked it up and read the note.

"Tony, I hope you find this. I've been abducted by three men. I will try to escape. I hope to see you soon." It was signed "Love, Cassie." Tony's name and phone number were at the bottom. Tony recognized Cassie's handwriting. "I wonder why she wrote "3" then crossed it out and made it "2." And why write my contact info on a note to me?" Tony wondered aloud.

"She probably hoped if someone else found it, they would call you, so you'd find out what happened. Pretty smart on her part."

"Shit, I was afraid it might be something like this," Tony said.

"Tony, this is a good sign. At least we know she was here and planning an escape. She had to have enough freedom to write the note. That's good. It means she's okay."

Now that they knew she'd been abducted, they needed to get the police involved. As they walked out of the mine Tony asked, "If we call the police won't they want us to stay here and answer their questions? I realize we need to call them, but I'm afraid they'll stop us from searching, at least for a while. Cassie might not have that much time."

"I know you're worried, but we need to think this through and do whatever will be the most likely to help Cassie. We need to get the police involved. We aren't armed and depending on the meaning of Cassie's note, we may be outnumbered. I'll call the police and conveniently fail to mention that you're with me. If they push the issue of waiting here until help arrives, you can continue the search. I'll wait here and get them up-to-speed. Does that sound like a plan you can live with?"

"I guess so. I don't like the idea of us splitting up, but if you think that's the best plan, I'll go along."

They scrambled to the top of the ridge where there might be cell service. The height of the ridgeline not only allowed them to place a call to the police, but also gave them a view of the surrounding area in every direction. Far off to the east they saw Cassie trudging slowly toward them. Her head bent forward, she was barely moving. Tony blew his whistle. Rob had taken out binoculars and watched Cassie. She looked toward them.

"How does she look?" Tony asked.

"She looks pretty banged up, but she's moving. She sees us."

Cassie was sure it must be a hallucination. Tony and Rob were standing on the ridge above the mine waving. She desperately wanted to run to them, but she couldn't. She was barely able to keep moving forward. It took every bit of strength she possessed not to stop right there, sit down, and wait for them to come to her.

The two men ran down to meet her. Cassie collapsed in Tony's arms. They helped her back into the shade of the mine. Tony tended to Cassie's head wound and got her to drink some water. In addition to the cut on her head, she was sunburned and had some obvious bruises. She needed to rest for a bit before they started the hike back to the ATVs.

Cassie wanted to tell them what had happened, but she was very tired. Tony suggested she hold off until they met the police at the hospital in town. He knew she'd have to go through it all in detail then. To be honest, looking at Cassie's condition, he wasn't sure he was ready to hear the details of her ordeal.

They rested for an hour or so and let Cassie drink as much water as she wanted. With her head injury, they needed to keep her awake. It felt like they were torturing her, she was so tired.

While she was resting, Rob climbed the ridge and called Sue. He told her they had found Cassie safe and would be heading back to the house. He also called the police and reported what had happened and asked them to send someone to the hospital later to take her statement.

The hike back to the ATV's was slow with both men taking turns helping Cassie. They had to take frequent rest stops, but they made it. With Cassie situated in her ATV's passenger seat, they headed back to Rob's.

CHAPTER SIX

At the hospital, Cassie was treated for severe sunburn and mild dehydration. They cleaned the cut on her head and sutured it with eighteen stitches. She had a lot of cuts and bruises, but time would heal those. They kept her overnight for observation due to the concussion. When she awoke, Tony was dozing in the chair beside her bed. He explained that the police would be stopping by to take her statement.

Later that evening, when the police showed up at the hospital, she told them everything that had happened. Tony was horrified to hear what she had endured but was glad it wasn't worse. He tried hard to keep his anger under control. When the policeman asked Cassie to go through the story again from the beginning, Tony had to excuse himself. He couldn't take hearing it again. He went to get coffee and didn't go back into the room until the policeman was wrapping up. After a few final clarifications, the officer explained that Cassie would need to come by the police station, when she was released from the hospital, to sign her statement and pinpoint the spots on the map where one of her captors was bitten by the rattler and where she had shot the other.

"Just to recap, you were abducted at gunpoint, left a snake bite victim to die, stabbed a man with a chisel, and shot another man. Are those the highlights?" he asked. Something in the cop's tone pissed Tony off.

Cassie nodded. The policeman asked to speak with Tony in the hallway.

"Mr. Bennett, I have to tell you, her story is pretty unbelievable. We'll have someone check out the locations after she marks them on the map for us, but I'd suggest you let the doctors know that she might not have a grasp on reality," the policeman told him. "Confusion is normal with a grade three concussion."

Tony was livid. "Officer, did you get a look at the condition she's in. It's pretty clear that someone assaulted her. You can see the handprints on her arms for god's sake. I assure you that she told you exactly what happened. I'm sure you'll find corroborating evidence when you check out those locations."

"Look, Mr. Bennett, I don't mean any disrespect, but you have to admit her story is pretty unbelievable."

"Not if you know Cassie," Tony said and went back to her bedside.

"What did he want to tell you that he wasn't willing to say in front of me?" Cassie asked.

Tony took a deep breath trying to ease his anger. "He wanted to make sure I knew how important it was for you to come by the station when you're released."

Cassie was exhausted. Tony offered to stay with her, but she told him she was going to sleep. He kissed her good night and told her he'd be back in the morning. She was asleep before he reached the hallway.

X X X

When Cassie awoke the next morning, she felt much better. After a quick shower and clean clothes, she was feeling more like herself. The doctor checked her injuries and released her. Tony stopped at her favorite breakfast spot. When the food arrived, she realized she was starving. She had eaten little in the last two days. The police station was the next stop. They met the officer who had taken Cassie's statement at the hospital. She sensed some tension between Tony and the officer, but maybe she was just imagining things. She was still very tired.

She signed the required documents and marked on a topographical map the spots where the events took place, as best as she could remember. By the time Tony got her back to her condo, she was exhausted both mentally and physically.

"I can't believe this all happened in just one weekend. It seemed like days and days," Cassie said as she collapsed on the sofa.

"It's been a long couple of days. I called Bob and explained what happened without going into too much detail. He'll stop by tomorrow to check on you."

"That's good. Honestly, right now, I'm exhausted, but I want to get back to work as soon as possible. If I rest for a day or two, I should be good to go."

"Do you want me to call your Mom to see if she can come out to take care of you?"

"Definitely not. I'm not sure if I'll even tell her what happened. I'll be fine. I promise. I just need to sleep."

Tony made her comfortable on the sofa, and she slept until early evening, waking only long enough to eat a light dinner before falling asleep again. He covered her up and let her sleep where she was until morning. She woke briefly when she heard him in the kitchen. She told him she was feeling better and he should go to work.

Tony called Bob to make sure he was going to come by and check on Cassie. He doubted he'd be able to concentrate on work, but he knew Cassie hated to be taken care of, so he would try to abide by her wishes.

CHAPTER SEVEN

When Bob let himself in with the spare key Cassie had given him, she was still sleeping on the sofa. It nearly broke his heart to see how bad she looked. She had a big gash on her head, and her arms had purple bruises that looked like handprints. She was like a daughter to him, and he couldn't imagine why anyone would do this to her. As he was watching her sleep, she opened her eyes and smiled a weak smile.

"Hi, Bob. Tony said you'd stop by today. I'm glad to see you." She pushed herself up to a sitting position with a grimace that didn't go unnoticed.

Bob asked what he could do to help her. She told him she needed coffee. She told him about the tracks she found in the desert but avoided telling him anything else about what had happened. The look on his face told her that Tony had already explained more than she intended to share. She let him know she wanted to go back to work the next day. He insisted on picking her up. He made her some soup and another cup of coffee before leaving her to rest. He knew that hovering over her, which is all he wanted to do, would only make her angry.

X X X

Cassie was still exhausted the next day but was glad to get some normalcy back into her life. Bob picked her up and drove her to the office. She knew that she would spend most of the day telling her co-workers about her ordeal. She gave a full statement to her BLM supervisor, trying to stick to the facts and leave out as much drama as possible. She knew from Cory's questions and comments that he'd already seen the police report. Since the incident happened primarily on BLM land, they were technically in charge of the investigation.

Late that afternoon, the policeman who had taken her statement stopped by the office to talk with her. They had found the snakebite victim dead where she had told them he'd be. They found a second body, the man she shot in the leg, near the area she had indicated. Her shot had hit the femoral artery, and he'd bled out where he fell.

X X X

Bob dropped her off at home and made sure she had everything she needed for the night. She enjoyed a cup of her favorite Italian roast coffee while catching up on email and fell asleep on the sofa before seven. Tony stopped by to check on her, but she didn't even wake up. He left a note, which she found in the morning.

The remainder of the work week passed without incident. Cassie's coworkers were shocked by what had happened and how well Cassie was handling it. They provided distractions when she seemed to be dwelling on it too much. Tony kept very close tabs on her, and while she appreciated his support, she knew she'd need to feel like things were back to normal again soon. She needed to be back in control of her life.

The following weekend, Cassie was still feeling exhausted, so she spent a quiet weekend at home. Over coffee with Tony on Sunday morning, she said, "I've been thinking about those weird tracks I saw in the desert when I was trying to get back to the ATV. My mind wasn't exactly clear at that point, but I know they were unusual. I'd like to check them out further and see if we might be able to track whatever made them. Maybe we can take the ATV out next weekend."

"Sure, if you feel up to it," Tony said, "but after what happened, I'd think you'd want to avoid going back out there."

Irritated, Cassie replied, "I can't avoid it Tony. It's my job, and I love the desert. I refuse to let one bad experience ruin that for me."

"I'd hardly call what you went through a 'bad experience'. You could have died out there, Cass. I was worried sick. You're damn lucky that things worked out the way they did. You're tough, Cassie, but you're not indestructible. You need to take this seriously."

"I am taking it seriously. I'm fine, and I want my life to get back to normal."

She'd drawn a line in the sand and Tony knew not to cross it. He was concerned about taking Cassie back into the desert so soon, thinking it might bring back too many bad memories and set back her recovery. He tried to talk her out of it all week, but if he didn't go with her, she'd go alone. He wasn't going to let that happen no matter how angry he was with her.

Cassie firmly believed that the only way to overcome fear was to face it head-on, and he could tell that she was determined not to be afraid to be in the desert. Tony explained the situation to Rob and Sue. They shared his concerns about Cassie, and they agreed to go with them to search for the tracks. They were interested in what Cassie had found, but they mainly went along to provide moral support.

X X X

With only minimal backtracking, Cassie was able to lead them to the tracks. They were still visible, though just barely, and everyone agreed that they were not something any of them could identify. Cassie took lots of photos and measurements to pass along to her supervisor. She made note of the GPS coordinates, so they could mark it on a map of the area. The desert was as quiet as usual, and they encountered no other people. Cassie seemed nervous and frequently looked over her shoulder. She hated feeling afraid of anything.

X X X

Cassie's life was returning to normal. The fact that Tony, and everyone else who knew what had happened, seemed to hover a bit more was beginning to grate on Cassie's nerves. Tony acted like he'd been more impacted by her ordeal than she had. She knew she should be happy that he cared for her that much, but she was starting to feel trapped. She had learned in the past few years that she never dealt well with feeling trapped whether that was in a situation, a job, or a relationship. Even at work, the other rangers found reasons to keep her in the office. She wasn't reacting well to everyone being over-protective of her. She was losing her patience and starting to bristle. Thankfully, Bob knew that she needed to feel like she was in control. He kept a closer eye on her than usual but was careful not to make it obvious.

X X X

Cassie was eating leftover Chinese food one evening while checking her email when she realized she was staring at a drawing she'd made of the tracks. *That looks a lot like a larger version of a roadrunner track,* she thought. She found her desert track book and opened it to the roadrunner page. She compared the tracks she found to the photos in the book and, other than size, they appeared to be identical.

The roadrunner is a common bird in the Desert Southwest. It's a member of the cuckoo family. Roadrunners can fly but

28

seldom do. They prefer to run down their prey. It isn't unusual to find roadrunner tracks in the desert around Las Cruces. Unlike most bird tracks which are three-toed, roadrunner tracks are 4-toed, and form an "X" with two toes facing front and two facing the rear.

Cassie mentioned to Bob that she had realized the tracks looked like giant roadrunner tracks. "They do look like that," Bob agreed, "but that would be one hell of a roadrunner. To have feet that big it would have to be huge. I sure wouldn't want to run across something like that when we're out on patrol."

CHAPTER EIGHT

Once it was clear that Cassie was suffering no obvious ill effects from her abduction, her boss asked her if she was up to leading some of her fellow rangers out to where she found the tracks. Cassie's co-workers had taken an interest in the pictures she tacked up on her cubicle wall. She made sure she took a pair of binoculars in her pack along with her usual desert gear. Once at the site, Cassie played tour guide, and soon the group was busy taking photos and measurements and looking for more prints.

Cassie walked a short distance away to find some quiet and rest for a bit. Being back in the area again was taking more of a mental toll than she expected. She found a spot on the backside of the rock wall that sheltered the tracks and sat down to relax and gather her thoughts. After eating a granola bar and drinking a bottle of water, she stood and stretched, preparing to rejoin the group. She turned in a complete circle surveying her surroundings. As she did so, she noticed a ridgeline to the east. She was scanning the ridge, mentally cataloging its features to use as a landmark in future explorations, when she detected movement. She was sure she saw something moving out there, but she couldn't tell what it was.

Cassie pulled out her binoculars and scanned the distant ridge. There was something out there, but she was too far away to identify it. She called Bob over to have a look.

After a few minutes, Bob said, "You know, Cassie, I'll be honest with you, I thought maybe you were just spooked being out here again, but something is moving behind that first ridge line. Even with the binoculars, I haven't been able to figure out what it is. If you're up for it, we should come back tomorrow and explore that area," Bob told her as he passed her the binoculars. Cassie scanned the ridgeline but saw nothing.

X X X

The next day, Bob and Cassie headed out to the spot where they'd seen movement the day before. They drove to the end of the dirt road and then set out for the distant ridge on foot. They stopped regularly for water and to scout their surroundings with binoculars. They saw nothing for a while, but during one of their stops, Bob spotted something moving behind the eastern-most ridge. He passed the binoculars to Cassie.

"I see something but only the top of a head or the back of something. It's moving along the ridgeline," Cassie said passing the binoculars back to Bob. "Let's keep going. Maybe we can get closer."

Once they had scrambled up the ridge, they realized there was a deep arroyo between the first and second ridges.

"It might be a Desert Big Horn Sheep. They could easily be walking along the backside of that ridge and we might only see their shoulders or head," Bob said.

"Maybe, but it seemed bigger. Lots bigger," mused Cassie.

Something in the valley below caught their attention, and they both looked that way. Quietly, Cassie put the binoculars to her eyes. "Oh my God!" she exclaimed. "What the hell am I looking at?" She passed the binoculars to Bob. "It can't be what it looks like."

"What it looks like to me is a giant turkey vulture with roadrunner feet," Bob said.

Taking back the binoculars, Cassie looked closely at the feet of the beast. They watched the bird as it walked along the base of the ridge, partially hidden by mesquite. Suddenly, it turned in their direction, sniffed the air, and let out a loud clicking noise. They fought the urge to run and remained perfectly still. After what seemed like hours, but was really only a few seconds, the creature turned and headed back along the ridge away from Bob and Cassie. They stayed put for several minutes without speaking. Eventually, Cassie broke the silence. "We didn't take any pictures did we? No one will believe us. You did see the same thing I did, didn't you?"

Bob removed his sunglasses and rubbed his eyes. "If you saw a turkey vulture the size of a house, then, yep, I'm right with you. I never thought those Thunderbird legends were based on reality, but now I'm not so sure."

They sat staring after the creature a few minutes before heading back down the ridge. They returned to the SUV in silence, each glancing frequently over their shoulders.

Once at the vehicle, neither one seemed to want to talk about what they had seen for fear they might have imagined it. When they were nearly back to the office, Bob said, "You know we have to report it, right?"

"I know," admitted Cassie. "Can we hold off a day or two? I need some time to be sure we're prepared for how this might be received. I need to adjust my idea of reality."

"There's no way this is a joke, is it?

"I can't think of any way, but that's why I want to consider the ramifications before we submit our report. Let's put a hold on it for twenty-four hours?"

"Sure. Tomorrow's my day off anyway. Let's meet for breakfast Thursday before work and figure out what we want to do."

CHAPTER NINE

When Cassie got home from work, she couldn't think straight. Her brain kept replaying what she'd seen like it was on an endless loop. She knew how crazy it would sound if she told someone about it. She decided to tell Tony and use his reaction to gauge how other people might react.

That night over pizza, Cassie told Tony what she and Bob had seen. He was skeptical which really pissed her off. He, of all people, should know her well enough to know that she wouldn't make this up. She certainly didn't have hallucinations.

"It's just hard to believe something that large hasn't been seen before. I know that section of the desert is pretty remote," Tony admitted. "We spend a lot of time out there, and we've never explored that specific area before. Maybe there are just too few people out there to run across this thing. Probably, those who do think they're hallucinating from dehydration or heat exhaustion."

"Maybe it has been seen. Every year we get reports that someone has spotted the legendary Thunderbird. Maybe they really did. I feel like my world has been turned upside down. I thought my run-in with those men in the desert would change my life, but now, finding the tracks and seeing that bird, I feel like I've lost my grasp on reality."

"I understand. You've been through a lot these past few weeks. Maybe you should see a therapist or something."

"I'll admit I'm holding on to reality by a very thin thread. No, that's not really true. It's more like I'm not even sure what reality is anymore, but I'm not in need of psychiatric help just yet."

X X X

Cassie and Bob both realized reporting the sighting would cause some people to question their sanity. They hoped their reputations and the fact that both of them saw the same thing, would lend credibility to the report. Over breakfast, they discussed options and talked about what they thought might happen when people found out about the Thunderbird. They had lots of concerns, but in the end, they decided they would report the sighting to their supervisor in person, rather than preparing a written report. They planned to ask Cory to keep the information private until they had a chance to gather photographic evidence of the bird.

X X X

When Bob and Cassie explained the situation to Cory, he admitted it was difficult to believe but said he couldn't imagine two more unlikely people to report something like that unless it was real. He still hoped they might be mistaken and what they had seen might not be as strange as it seemed. There might be some logical explanation, though he couldn't come up with one. He assigned them to patrol the area where they had seen the bird for the next week. Hopefully, they would spot the creature again and be able to take pictures. The three of them agreed no written report of the sighting would be prepared, and no one other than the three of them, and Tony, would know about it until they saw what the week ahead produced.

Neither Cassie nor Bob could remember ever being so excited to go on patrol. They checked out two digital cameras from BLM inventory and made sure they had plenty of batteries.

Bob and Cassie made a conscious decision to suspend the unreality of the situation and accept that they had seen the giant bird. Doubts still surfaced from time to time, but they were quickly overridden by the knowledge that they were both sane, rational people and had seen the same thing. They also shored up their resolve with the knowledge that the tracks Cassie found in the desert had been made by the creature they saw or some close relative. They decided to refer to the creature as a Thunderbird. They had no idea if that was scientifically accurate, but it seemed to fit the current evidence.

CHAPTER TEN

Cassie and Bob drove as close to the ridgeline as possible, loaded the gear into their packs, and headed off. The sun was bright, and the thermometer had already topped ninety degrees. When they reached the western-most ridge, they climbed to the top and settled in to scan the arroyo below. Each of them had a pair of high-powered binoculars focused on the valley floor.

As with most ventures of this type, the adrenaline of the hunt waned as the hours passed with no sightings. After a while they hadn't spotted anything, so they headed off to explore the next ridgeline to the east. They walked down into the arroyo and crossed to the next line of rocks. They kept their eyes peeled for tracks but the sandy soil didn't hold prints for long. When they reached the other side, they had to scramble up a rock face to reach the top of the next ridge.

They settled in to monitor the desert below. Just as Cassie was getting restless, Bob pointed to the next ridge. He leaned over and whispered to her, "Look at the next ridgeline about twenty degrees south of our position. I think something moved over there."

Cassie and Bob both scanned the area for several minutes but saw nothing. They headed down again, crossed another arroyo and scrambled up another rock face. They decided to walk along the ridgeline to the spot where Bob had seen movement. They settled in and watched but saw nothing.

Dejected, but still committed to the search, they took a different trail back in hopes that they might discover some scat or prints that they missed earlier. By the time they came to the original valley, they were tired and disappointed. Bob stopped so suddenly Cassie nearly ran into him.

He pointed under a thick stand of mesquite at an area that was a little muddy. Water seeping out of an underground spring and the shade of the trees kept the ground damp. Clearly displayed in the mud was a huge X-shaped print similar to those Cassie had found before. Since this one was in the mud, it was better defined. After taking numerous photos and measuring everything imaginable, they noted the GPS coordinates and headed back to the office.

X X X

The next day Bob and Cassie got an earlier start to have as much time as possible to search for the bird. They met at 6:00 AM and hit the drive thru for breakfast on the way to the desert. They explored the same area as the previous day, taking a more northerly route across the ridges and arroyos. They didn't take a serious break until they reached the top of the furthest ridge they had explored the day before. They settled in to scan the arroyo below and enjoy the sandwiches Cassie had packed. They spotted nothing and were packing up the remains of their lunch when Cassie held up her hand to stop Bob from talking. She pointed to the arroyo north of their location. Even without binoculars they could both clearly see it.

Bob kept watch while Cassie retrieved the longest lens they had and set up the camera and tripod. She wanted as many good shots as she could get. She set the timer to take a shot every ten seconds. She and Bob stood and watched the bird walk slowly along the base of the next ridge to the east. When it was almost directly below them, it raised its head and sniffed the air. Cassie and Bob held their collective breaths not wanting to startle it but suspecting it had caught their scent. After what seemed like hours, the Thunderbird continued down the arroyo heading south. Cassie adjusted the camera to follow the bird until it was out of sight.

Neither of them moved. They didn't want to break the spell. Bob eventually spoke. "I'd say we have pretty well confirmed that we aren't crazy. The creature does exist, and now we've got the pictures to prove it."

They were within sight of the SUV before Bob spoke again. "Don't take this the wrong way, but I still can't believe what we saw. I know we found the fresh track yesterday, but it's such a shock to realize it really does exist."

"I understand," said Cassie. "I'm trying to decide whether I'm happier to know we have proof or just to know that I'm not crazy."

CHAPTER ELEVEN

During the remainder of their workweek, Cassie and Bob spotted the bird two more times, both in the same area as the first sighting. During their three encounters with the bird, she and Bob took over a thousand photographs. She knew some of the pics would be good. She hadn't had time to look at them all yet, but just looking at the first few photos, she knew they had the proof they needed.

When Cory saw the photos, he was shocked. "Don't take this the wrong way, but I still can't believe these photos. It's not that I didn't believe you, but still, it's a shock to realize that it really does exist."

"I understand," said Cassie. "I still find it pretty hard to believe myself."

They spoke at length about what they were required to do as BLM rangers and what they might want to do us private citizens. They were required to report anything unusual spotted during routine patrols. One option was for them to write their reports making only minor mention of having seen something unusual and filing the reports as normal. With any luck no one up the chain would notice, and they could pretend this never happened.

"While I appreciate the potential advantage to us and the creature of keeping it secret, I'm not sure I'm prepared to pretend we didn't see it," Cassie explained. If we saw the bird, someone else will too. Could it pose any threat to humans? If so, then we have to come up with a plan to deal with it because if something happens and then it comes out that we knew about it, we'd be in serious trouble."

"You're right, of course," said Cory. "Guess I was hoping for an easy way out, but I doubt that will be possible. The area where you ran into the bird is not that far from some popular hiking trails. Sooner or later, the creature is going to come into contact with other humans, if it hasn't already. It's our job to make sure that interaction brings no harm to either side."

"Can we have a few more days to think this over before we decide how to move forward?" Cassie asked.

"I don't see why not. Let's take a few more days to figure out how to handle this information for the good of all involved, both human and animal," Cory agreed.

That night over dinner, Cassie explained the situation to Tony. She had kept him up-to-date with her sightings, and he'd seen the photos. She had assumed Cory would tell them what they had to do, so she really hadn't considered how she'd like to handle it. Now that it seemed she might have some say in the matter, she wanted to discuss it with Tony and get his input.

"There's a lot to consider," Tony said. "If the sightings become public you'll have your fifteen minutes of fame and might make some money from selling your story or photographs, but some folks will be skeptical and brand you as crazy. That might be tough to take and may hurt your career. How are you going to handle that?"

"Gee, I hadn't considered what would happen if the information became public. I'd been worried about it spreading to everyone at BLM, but you're right," Cassie said, "If it goes outside of just you, I, Bob, and Cory then it's likely the public will learn about it somehow."

"You really need to think about this, Cass. This kind of thing can change your life, and not for the better."

"You're right, I guess," Cassie said. She felt finding the creature was something great that she should be proud of, not something that would lead to her being branded as a "crazy person" and destroy her life. Surely Tony was just pointing out the worst case scenario. It made her sad to think she lived in a world where discovering a new species was seen as a bad thing. She'd talk to Bob and get his input on what they should do.

Cassie decided while she was analyzing things and making decisions, she should also make some decisions about her relationship with Tony. They'd been together for a long time. At one time, she dreamed of a happily ever after with Tony, but that was before she had enough life experience to realize that fairy tales don't always work out well in the real world. She and Tony had grown apart. It happened. They wanted different things out of life. Both of them realized something needed to change, but they still cared about each other and neither wanted to be the one to end the relationship.

Cassie's abduction made her take stock of her life in a way she had never done before. Tony didn't make her happy. He wasn't going to change and neither was she. It was time to close that chapter of her life and move on.

X X X

Cassie made plans to have dinner with Bob to discuss what they wanted to do about their discovery. Cassie was aware they would both have to live with the decisions they made.

Three hours of dinner, coffee, desert, and what-ifs finally led to a plan. They wanted to find out what the BLM could do to protect the Thunderbirds. Once protections were in place, they wanted to share their find publicly. They explained their plan to Cory and he started making calls to BLM's sister agencies seeking support. He contacted a friend with the Fish and Wildlife Service, and started things in motion to list the bird as endangered.

Bob and Cassie prepared a press release to have ready when needed. Though they didn't plan to notify the media, they felt sure that as more people learned the story the likelihood of a leak increased. Cory called a meeting of the Las Cruces BLM office staff so that Cassie and Bob could present their discovery, and all the rangers could be prepared to protect the giant bird. And so the die was cast.

CHAPTER TWELVE

Much quicker than Cassie thought possible, someone leaked the story to the press. Cassie and Bob released their statement, and the insanity began in earnest. There were requests for interviews from local and national media outlets. They tried to stay low-key and not let it affect them, but that was nearly impossible. Waiting in line at the deli, Cassie was shocked to hear a young girl behind her whisper to her mother, "Isn't that the crazy lady that says she saw a giant bird in the desert?"

Experts at the BLM and FWS had validated Cassie's photos. Both organizations issued statements about the existence of the Thunderbird and their plans to protect it, but people still couldn't accept that it was true. Most people found it hard to believe that anything could remain undiscovered with current technology. Cell phones, remote cameras, and drones made it seem impossible that there could still be something left to discover. Cassie and Bob knew the truth.

People familiar with the Thunderbird legend believed that Cassie's discovery was the latest in a long line of reports about the giant bird from throughout the US and Canada. Many indigenous tribes have some type of Thunderbird legend. In most of those stories, the bird is said to be capable of creating great storms. Though the details differ, they agree that Thunderbirds are powerful and wrathful.

The first couple of weeks were the most difficult. After that, they still received a few requests for interviews or comments, and some people still considered them insane, but for the most part, their lives were getting back to normal.

One evening while eating dinner, Tony had a call from Rob saying that the search and rescue squad was meeting in the morning to assist in the search for a missing hiker in the Sacramento Mountains. "Do you want to come with us," he asked Cassie after he ended the call.

"I have to work, but BLM may send us out to participate anyway," she said.

X X X

Sure enough, when Cassie walked into the office Cory was asking for volunteers. Cassie and Bob volunteered and headed out to check in at the command post. Friends said that the hiker headed out two days before and never returned. Police found his vehicle at a popular trailhead and called for search and rescue. Teams with bloodhounds started down the trail and would report in if they found anything. The searchers were assigned areas in a grid pattern marked off on a topographic map. Cassie and Bob got an area they were familiar with which wasn't far from where they had discovered the Thunderbird.

At the noon check-in, no evidence of the hiker had been located. Bob and Cassie stopped for a lunch break and then resumed their search. A little after 2:00 PM, a call went out that the hiker's backpack had been found just north of Cassie and Bob's assigned quadrant. All searchers were asked to make their way to the coordinates where the gear was found, if they were close enough. Now that they knew where the man had been, they would concentrate the search in that location.

Bob checked the topo map and decided on a route that would take them to the new area. They gathered up their packs and headed out. It was another sunny hot day, but the searchers were well prepared. Everyone was determined to keep searching until darkness made it impossible. Cassie and Bob scrambled up a rocky slope and started down the other side when Bob called a halt. He spotted something in the arroyo. He took out the field glasses to get a better look.

"Look about a hundred yards to the right at the base of a mesquite bush," Bob said, passing the binoculars to Cassie.

"It could be a body." She sniffed the air. There was a faint odor. "Let's go check it out."

When they got closer, they could see that it was the remains of a young man. It was obvious he had been attacked by some type of animal. His clothes were shredded and punctured, and some pieces of the body were missing altogether. Cassie had to concentrate to suppress the bile that had risen in the back of her throat. She retreated a few feet upwind and tried to call the search coordinators but was unable to reach them on the radio. There was no cell service either.

They covered the body with a tarp and secured it with rocks. They continued on until they met up with the other searchers. Cassie and Bob reported what they had found and led the group back to the spot. No one could make a positive ID because of the condition of the remains, but they believed it was the missing hiker based on age, height, and hair color. The remains were transported to the Dona Ana County coroner's office in town, and the searchers returned to their normal lives.

The official cause of death was listed as an attack by an unknown animal. It took less than a day for the press to connect the death of the hiker to the discovery of the Thunderbird.

CHAPTER THIRTEEN

After avoiding Tony for a couple of weeks, Cassie realized she needed to put on her big girl panties and end the relationship so they both would be able to move on. She invited him over for dinner. After a pleasant meal and small talk about each other's week, Cassie told him that she wanted to breakup. As she expected, he wasn't very surprised or particularly upset. They both had seen it coming. He said he'd miss seeing her and hoped they could remain friends. She hugged him and closed the door behind him.

After shedding a few tears, she called her Mom to talk about the breakup.

"You don't seem very surprised," Cassie said.

"We always assumed you'd break up with Tony at some point. I know you two cared for each other, but it's been clear the past few years that he wasn't the man for you long term," her mom explained.

Cassie couldn't hide her surprise. "Did it ever occur to you to let me in on this?"

"Honey, we want you to make your own choices. We were sure you'd figure it out when you were ready to move on."

"I guess older and wiser wins again." She felt sad but knew it was the best decision for both she and Tony. Now she could move forward.

X X X

The media stuck with their story that the Thunderbird killed the hiker. Cassie hated to admit it, but she thought they were probably right. It wasn't fair that she and Bob were being vilified because they discovered the Thunderbird. No one knew enough about the bird to say for sure whether it was involved in the hiker's death. Two months ago, no one even knew it existed, so the body of knowledge was still pretty thin. The coroner's office, the BLM, and the FWS all issued statements saying that they had no evidence to indicate the bird was involved. Cassie had learned that when it came to the public, all you could do was issue a statement and let the chips fall where they may. She didn't like it, but she understood it was the reality of the current situation.

In spite of the turmoil in parts of her life, things were going great at work. Warning signs had been posted to remind everyone that the Thunderbird had been listed as an endangered species, and as such, killing it was illegal. Someone got lost in the desert and needed rescue at least once a week, but the rangers took it in stride.

Cassie spent a lot of time at the shooting range preparing for the US Championships. Currently ranked top five in the country, she wanted to make sure she maintained or improved her standing at this year's competition.

The BLM received notification that a team of researchers from FWS would be in town for the next several weeks to track and study the bird. They would be setting up camp on BLM land in the area where the bird had been discovered. They scheduled interviews with Bob and Cassie to hear their story firsthand. She was pleased to see that efforts to protect the bird were moving ahead so quickly.

She got a call from the police asking her to attend a line-up which might contain the only surviving member of the trio of men that kidnapped her. She thought she had put the incident behind her, but the phone call brought it all back, and that upset her. One of the men in the lineup was the tall guy who participated in her abduction. She was surprised by how angry it made her to see him again. Apparently, the experience had affected her more than she wanted to admit. After signing the required paperwork, the officer told her that someone would contact her if she had to testify. With so many charges against him, it would depend on how things were handled by the lawyers.

CHAPTER FOURTEEN

A week or so after the line-up, while she was eating dinner, there was a knock on Cassie's door. She looked through the peep hole and saw a policeman. She assumed the reason for his visit would be related to her case.

She opened the door, "What can I do for you, Officer?"

"I'm sorry to bother you, Ms. Carter. Have you seen Trevor Lewis in the past two days?" he asked.

"No. I haven't seen him recently. Is something wrong?"

"We're trying to locate him, ma'am. Thank you for your time." He turned and left.

Cassie called Mrs. Lewis to ask if everything was OK.

Trevor's Mom explained that Trevor didn't come home the previous day as scheduled. Trevor, his girlfriend, and another couple had gone for a hike in the desert the previous afternoon, and none of them returned. The police found Trevor's car parked at the university. They found the other missing boy's vehicle at the trailhead for Rabbit Ears Pass. Mrs. Lewis was frantic. Cassie told her that she would ask the other BLM rangers to keep an eye out for Trevor and his friends.

X X X

The next morning, Cassie told Cory about the missing students, and he made a request at the morning meeting to see if anyone had spotted the group. No one had. All the rangers were asked to be on the lookout for the kids. Cassie wondered why an official search hadn't been launched yet. She didn't understand how the police handled these things even though she'd been in this situation not too long ago herself.

By late afternoon, they received word that a formal search would be getting underway, and all available rangers were asked to participate. Neither Cassie nor Bob wanted to talk about the fact that the search area was in the same location as where they had found the Thunderbird. Each of them knew that the other noticed. It could just be a coincidence. That part of the desert was attracting a lot of attention lately because of the bird.

Cassie and Bob found nothing nor did any of the other teams. They stopped at the FWS researchers' campsite and ask if they had seen the missing hikers. They hadn't but said they'd keep an eye out for the students.

Cassie stopped to check on Mrs. Lewis on her way home. She understood that each passing hour must make it more difficult to expect a positive outcome. The only update on the situation was that one of Trevor's friends notified the police that he received a text from Trevor the day he went missing. The text said Trevor and his friends were heading out to get photos of the thunderbird.

Cassie knew it wasn't her fault, but she still felt responsible. If she hadn't found the bird none of this would be happening. She wrestled with it all night going back and forth between accepting that she was not at fault and blaming herself. She didn't sleep well. She called Bob and arranged to get an early start on the search. She intended to do everything she could to find the missing kids.

CHAPTER FIFTEEN

Rabbit Ears Pass is a highly visible landmark in the Organ Mountains outside Las Cruces. Its name comes from two stone spires that look like giant rabbit ears. There is an old mine in the area and the ruins of some old stone buildings. It's a popular hike in cool weather. Today the searchers were convening in the parking lot off Baylor Canyon Road. Cassie and Bob signed in and headed out. It was still relatively cool, in the low eighties, so the going was easier. They followed the main trail to the top of the pass before turning in a southeasterly direction. Cassie hoped they would find nothing. She wanted the kids found safe. She didn't think she could handle it if they found any evidence that implicated the Thunderbird.

Late in the afternoon a radio call went out saying Trevor and his girlfriend were found uninjured. Trevor couldn't provide any information as to what had happened to the other couple after they were separated. Cassie was relieved that Trevor and his friend were safe, but she worried about the two who remained missing. Search and rescue used the information Trevor provided to pinpoint the last spot where Marina and Tim were seen. That would be the starting point for the next day's search.

That evening Cassie went over to the Lewis' to see how they were doing. Trevor was sunburned and dehydrated but otherwise in good shape. Trevor's mom thanked Cassie for helping with the search and stopping by to check on them. Trevor told Cassie they hadn't seen the Thunderbird. At home, she printed out some of her photos of the birds and took them over to him.

X X X

She slept better knowing that at least two of the hikers came home safe. Cassie awoke early, so she headed to the shooting range before meeting Bob at the search command post. The starting point for the search activities had been moved to an area south of Dripping Springs. Bob and Cassie were able to drive into their assigned quadrant with the SUV, so they got a break from hiking.

Cassie had a bad feeling. As they scaled a small rocky ledge, Bob motioned for a stop. He pointed to the north, and sure enough, the Thunderbird was walking down the arroyo.

Neither could say why, but for some reason they decided to follow it. The bird didn't go far. They watched with binoculars as it headed south and disappeared behind a large rock formation. Cassie and Bob headed down into the valley to see if they could find it again. They had just reached the arroyo when the Thunderbird reappeared and headed back the way it had come. They both thought this might indicate that they had found the end of the bird's territory. Cassie suggested they check out where the bird disappeared. She hoped they'd learn why it turned around. "Could be where it's nest is located," Cassie said.

Nothing could have prepared her for what they found. As they passed through the vegetation at the base of the rocks, she saw a path. In a small clearing a few feet above the desert floor was a huge nest surrounded by prickly pear cactus. Finding the nest was a shock, but what was in the nest nearly caused Cassie to pass out. There was a person curled up in the fetal position. It was like a scene from some b-movie creature film, except it was real. At first, they both stood frozen by the scene and unable to decide what to do. They found an opening between the cactus plants and rushed to the body. Cassie knelt down beside it. After a closer look, she recognized the missing girl. She had blood on her face and arms, but she looked relatively unharmed. Cassie softly touched her arm, and the girl jerked awake and looked cautiously over her shoulder at them. Cassie saw the fear in her eyes. "Marina, we're here to help you. Are you injured? Can you move?" Cassie asked.

The girl slowly sat up. She looked around and lunged at Cassie, grabbing her in a hug. She broke down into uncontrolled sobs. When she calmed down, they assessed her injuries and found they were relatively minor. She could walk, so they helped her move away from the nest. They stayed as quiet as possible, and Bob kept an eye out for the bird while Cassie helped the girl up the rocky slope. Once they dropped down into the next valley, they took a break and asked the girl about her missing companion. She started to cry again.

Bob walked a short distance away, scrambled to the top of a rocky ledge where he had cell service, and called the searchers to let them know that they had found Marina and would be bringing her out to the checkpoint as quickly as possible. He told them once Marina was calmer she might be able to provide information about the location of the missing boy, but at this point, she was not able to do so.

Marina told Bob and Cassie that she and Tim were separated from Trevor and his girlfriend and wandered around the desert lost for a day. They had not seen the bird but found the nest, though they didn't realize what it was. It looked like a sheltered place to spend the night, and they were exhausted, so they got as comfortable as possible and quickly fell asleep. The bird came at dusk. Marina awoke to it pecking her arm and nudging her with its head. She screamed which woke Tim. They tried to escape, but the bird put a foot on her and held her down.

Tim tried to help her, but every time he got close, the bird snapped at him and forced him away. After doing this for what seemed like hours, Tim decided to go for help. It didn't seem like the bird wanted to hurt her, but it didn't want her to move. They thought if she stayed quiet, she'd be able to sneak away once the creature left or went to sleep.

Marina said she tried to stay awake but had trouble breathing. "I think maybe some of my ribs are cracked," she explained. "I just sat there and tried not to move or make a sound. The bird watched me for a while and seemed to be settling down. I tried to crawl away a little bit at a time, but then the damn thing put her head on me and I was trapped. I wanted to stay awake in case I got a chance to get free, but I guess I fell asleep. I didn't wake up 'til you found me."

"Do you have any idea what direction Tim was headed?" Bob asked.

"He headed over the rocks behind the nest, but I couldn't see which way he went from there," Marina said.

They helped her back to the SUV and headed for the checkpoint. Bob radioed ahead to have an ambulance waiting to take Marina to the hospital. He also passed along the coordinates of Tim's last known location. Bob and Cassie headed home, hoping that the searchers would find Tim safe and sound. Unfortunately, when Tim was found he was neither safe nor sound. The searchers who found the body said he had obviously been attacked by something large. Cassie knew what had attacked Tim, even though she hoped she was wrong.

She wasn't. The coroner confirmed the attack marks matched pictures he had seen of the Thunderbird.

The public was incensed. How could the government protect this killer? How could they let people into the area where they knew this killer lived? It was just like what happens when someone is attacked by a bear in a national park. The big twist to this story was the complication that this might be the last bird of its kind. Science wanted to capture and study it, while the public wanted to see it hunted down.

It was a tough few weeks for Cassie and Bob. Cassie knew this too would pass and it did.

CHAPTER SIXTEEN

The finger pointing and accusations subsided, and life slowly returned to normal. Cassie was in no rush to get back into the dating scene. She wanted to take some time for herself. She realized she hadn't been truly on her own since her second year in college. She believed things happened when they were meant to happen and that was fine by her. Most evenings found her editing her photos of the thunderbirds. On weekends, she spent as much time as possible at the shooting range.

A few days later, she and Bob had just returned from patrolling the Rabbit Ears Pass area when Cory leaned out of his office door and called, "Cassie, can you come in here for a moment?" Cassie hoped that all the press around her discovery of the Thunderbird was not going to get her into trouble with the BLM. She loved her job and couldn't imagine doing anything else.

After Cassie took a seat, Cory said, "How are you doing these days? Your life's been a bit hectic lately."

"I'm doing fine. Thanks for asking. I'm glad to be back to my regular patrol duties."

"I called you in because I just received an email asking that I send you to Montana to represent the Southwest region in the BLM Competitive Shoot Out. Is that something you'd be interested in?" Cory asked, knowing full well that the only thing Cassie enjoyed more than roaming around the desert was competitive shooting.

"That's a surprise. Absolutely. I'd be honored."

"I'll forward you all the details. Grace can make your travel arrangements. Go and make us all proud," Cory said as he showed her to the door.

Cassie returned to her desk a bit amazed. This was a dream come true. A shooting competition that she didn't have to pay to attend or take vacation time for. *What more could a girl ask for*, she thought to herself.

She printed out the details and learned that the trip was only a few days away. She'd need to hit the range as much as possible between now and then. Cassie loved shooting, but since her ordeal in the dessert, she'd had little time to practice. Perhaps it would be good to have a diversion after all the recent insanity in her life.

X X X

When Cassie arrived in Montana, she retrieved her luggage and took the shuttle to the hotel. She settled in and unpacked. According to her itinerary, there were no events scheduled until the following morning when the first practice round would take place. Cassie had received an email with instructions that someone would meet her in the lobby at 7:00 AM to take her to the competition range. She looked at her fellow diners while she ate dinner in the hotel restaurant. She assumed all of the out-of-town competitors were staying at the same hotel, but she doubted she'd recognize any of them. The Bureau of Land Management was a large organization. Once you'd been in it for a while you had the opportunity to transfer to different offices and get to know other rangers, but she hadn't met much of anyone except a few rangers from the surrounding BLM sites in New Mexico. She ate well and slept well, though she was excited for the competition to get started.

Cassie got up early. She showered and enjoyed breakfast downstairs, then went back to her room, brewed a cup of her favorite Italian roast coffee, packed up her gear, and was waiting in the lobby. There were a few other people who seemed to be waiting for someone, but they were all in business attire, and Cassie didn't think they were her fellow competitors. An attractive man wearing khakis and a green polo shirt with the insignia BITES on it walked through the front door. He moved directly to Cassie and stuck out his hand.

"Hello, Ms. Carter. It's nice to meet you. I'm Hank Smithfield," he said as they shook hands. "Is this all of your gear?"

"It's nice to meet you too, Mr. Smithfield. Yes, this is all I need," Cassie replied, pointing to her rifle case and backpack.

Hank picked up her backpack and headed for the door. They stowed her gear in the back of a black SUV, and he held the passenger door open for her. After Cassie climbed in, he closed the door and walked around to the driver's side. Hank got in and fastened his seatbelt. Cassie asked, "Aren't you picking up other contestants?"

"My list had only your name on it. Perhaps the others made different arrangements."

Cassie used to be a very trusting soul, but sadly, that had changed since her abduction. She was more cautious about people. It wouldn't make sense for the BLM to send someone to pick her up when there should be other competitors staying at the same hotel that needed a ride.

"How did you know who I was?" Cassie asked, realizing that he had come up to her as though he knew her.

"They showed me your photo," Hank explained.

"I'm sorry, Hank, but could you show me some identification, please?" she asked.

"Sure. No problem." He flipped open a credential wallet with a Homeland Security badge. "Do you want to see my driver's license, too?" he asked.

"That won't be necessary. I'm here for a BLM competition. Why is Homeland Security involved?"

"We're helping out because a lot of the local BLM staffers are up north assisting with a forest fire."

"OK. I'm ready to go." Cassie told him. Maybe she should explain the reason for her suspicious nature, but she wasn't going to share that much of her personal life with a stranger. She still thought it odd that none of the other competitors were going with them, but Hank's credentials appeared to be authentic.

They had been driving in silence for nearly an hour, and Cassie got nervous again. "I didn't realize the competition was being held so far from the hotel," she said casually.

"It's quite a ways out of the city. Can't have any stray bullets hitting the public," Hank said.

Cassie got out her cell phone and pretended to check messages. In reality, she was trying to access a map and determine her current location. "No bars," she complained.

"Yeah, the service out here in the mountains is spotty at best. It won't be a problem once we get to the lodge."

CHAPTER SEVENTEEN

Cassie grew more and more apprehensive. She'd never had a panic attack and wasn't sure what they felt like, but she thought she might be on the verge of one.

A few minutes later, Hank turned off the highway into a dirt road heading further into the mountains. Cassie nearly lost it. They had to be going to some secret hideout somewhere. She knew it was crazy to feel that way when a Homeland Security agent was with her, but she couldn't stop her mind from replaying scenes from a million bad horror movies that all took place in some remote cabin in the woods. She tried to calm her breathing, but she wasn't succeeding. She clutched the armrest so tightly she thought it would leave permanent indentations. *Oh well, maybe the police can get my prints from the armrest and use them to identify my body,* she thought.

After several more turns, they came into a clearing with a huge lodge in the center. It was beautiful. It was all log and had a porch across the front. Definitely not the dark, dreary ramshackle hideout she'd been imagining. She smiled. A few black SUVs were parked in the driveway, some with the same BITES logo as on Hank's shirt.

Cassie breathed a sigh of relief. *This looks more like what I expected*, she thought to herself. "It seems awfully mountainous for a shooting competition, but perhaps there's more flat ground behind the lodge," she said as she climbed from the SUV and went around back to retrieve her gear.

"Hank, I see the BITES logo on the cars the same as on your shirt. What does it stand for?" she asked as she walked toward the stairs.

"Um....It's the name of a local catering company that's sponsoring the event," he said.

A few men dressed just like HANK sat on the lodge porch. It seemed strange that the sponsor's logo hadn't been on any of the correspondence she'd received. He led her into a welcoming room centered by a massive fieldstone fireplace.

"Is there an event schedule posted somewhere?" Cassie asked. She was a seasoned competitor and knew how these things normally worked.

Hank didn't answer. He escorted her to a sitting area. She had made it difficult for him to maintain the secrecy he'd been told was necessary. He told her to have a seat. While she waited, which was strange in itself, she noticed that all of the people she could see were men. That wasn't odd. Though there were many female BLM rangers these days, it was still a small percentage of the total. Since she was here for a shooting competition that would drop the number of women even lower, but it seemed unusual that she didn't see even one other women. Most shooting competitions had men's and women's divisions though perhaps the BLM had decided to combine them.

Hank returned followed by an older gentleman dressed in an impeccably tailored business suit and tie. Hank introduced him as Mr. Meecham, and he shook hands with Cassie.

"It's nice to meet you, Ms. Carter. Please follow me to my office," he said as he headed back the way he had come. She wondered why everyone she'd seen in a uniform had the BITES logo. She'd seen no one in a BLM uniform.

Cassie hurried to pick up her gear and follow him. He led her past a library, a conference room, a large kitchen and dining room, and several offices. He opened the door with his nameplate on it to allow Cassie to enter. The office was nicely decorated in hunting lodge décor with a fireplace and the requisite moose head looming over the mantle. Large windows overlooked a beautiful mountain lake. Mr. Meecham motioned Cassie to one of the chairs in front of the desk and took his seat opposite her.

"The view is lovely, isn't it?" he commented.

"Yes, it is, but I don't see any sign of the competition range. Is it far from here?" She started to feel uneasy again. Patience might be a virtue but it was certainly not her strong suit. She had reached her limit. She was done playing games with these people, whoever they were.

She lifted the gun case onto her lap and opened the latches as she spoke. "Look, Mr. Meecham, I don't know who you work for or why I've been brought here, but I no longer believe this has anything to do with a BLM shooting competition. It's time you tell me what this is all about," Cassie said directly while loading a cartridge into the rifle.

"I assure you Ms. Carter there is no need for alarm. Please unload your weapon and return it to its case."

She held the firearm on her lap and just looked at him. Neither one of them blinked.

Finally, Mr. Meecham said, "Allow me to apologize for the secrecy, Ms. Carter. We would normally have taken the time to plan a much more clever way to introduce you to our organization, but time was of the essence. We wanted to take advantage of the BLM competition and perhaps did not think this through sufficiently."

"Who do you work for Mr. Meecham, and exactly why am I here?" Cassie demanded, holding the rifle calmly across her lap. She realized that she was not in a good position. Apparently, all the people she had seen worked with or for Mr. Meecham, and she was alone. Add to that the fact that she was miles from the city in an unfamiliar environment, and her options were pretty limited, but she had a weapon and ammo. They'd damn well tell her what was going on or she'd walk out with Mr. Meecham as a hostage, demand keys to a vehicle, and head back to town, where ever that was.

Though clearly shocked by Cassie's behavior, Mr. Meecham maintained his calm demeanor. Over the next two hours, he explained that he was the Field Operations Director for BITES, the Biological Investigation and Threat Eradication Service. The team was part of Homeland Security, but because they dealt with biological threats, normally in the form of animals of some description, they worked closely with the National Park Service, BLM, and FWS. They were a small agency with field agents, support staff, and a research lab.

He explained that the animals his teams encountered were not the wildlife she was used to dealing with at the BLM. They were animals that had either been created by human interference, as with genetic engineering or mutations caused by environmental poisons and things like that, or creatures long thought to be extinct. There were some that would remain myths until their existence was proven by hard evidence. Mr. Meecham explained that BLM rangers might handle a case about an aggressive grizzly bear while BITES would handle a case involving a Yeti.

CHAPTER EIGHTEEN

"BITES is basically the officially sanctioned US government organization charged with cryptid hunting," he said with a smile. "All of the creatures we hunt are unique and require very special handling."

"OK, I get it. You want me to tell you about the Thunderbird," Cassie said when Mr. Meecham reached the end of his explanation. "You could have just called or emailed me. You didn't have to go through this elaborate hoax. I'm afraid I didn't bring any photos along, but I can email them to you. What would you like to know?"

"Although I would like to discuss your amazing discovery with you at length, that is not why you're here today," he continued.

As he spoke, she unloaded the rifle and put it back into the case. She closed and latched the case and set it on the floor at her feet. Out of sight but not out of reach.

"I'm sorry, Mr. Meecham, but you must understand how this looked to me. I was picked up by someone who recognized me but whom I'd never met. I wondered why no other competitors where riding with us. Then the ride was much longer than seemed reasonable, and we turned off the highway onto a dirt road into the forest. I wasn't told why I was here or given any real information until now. I hope you can forgive my behavior. I was taken hostage by three men a few months ago and am still a bit overly cautious I'm afraid," Cassie explained.

"Oh, my dear. I had no idea. There was no mention of that in your files. I'm surprised it didn't show up on our police records scan though I suppose we don't look at cases were you would be listed as the victim. I hope you can forgive me. Had I known about that incident, I would never have taken the approach we did. I assure you we did not intend to cause you any discomfort."

"Wait. Why did you review my police records? What is it you want from me?"

"We want to offer you a job as a BITES agent."

"I'm sorry, did I hear you correctly? You want me to work for you?" Cassie asked, trying not to sound too incredulous.

"That's correct. We've been keeping track of your progress since you joined the BLM. It was originally your shooting ability that made you a "candidate of interest," as we call them," Mr. Meecham explained patiently. "When I learned about your discovery of the Thunderbird and how well you handled it, I knew you were ready to join BITES.

"One of the largest recruitment barriers we face is that so many people cannot admit that the creatures we focus on even exist. Past history has taught us that those candidates who are shown pictures of these creatures and say that they accept it, can still fall apart the first time they encounter a cryptid in the field. Your experience and abilities make you a perfect candidate to join our organization."

"I'm sorry, Mr. Meecham, this all seems like a sophisticated prank to me. Though I can't imagine who would go to this much trouble or why."

After more discussion and a tour of the facility, Cassie started to believe that there might be a very slim chance that this could be real, but it seemed unbelievable to her. It was much too elaborate a setup to be someone playing a joke on her, but she was still skeptical.

Cassie had several questions for Mr. Meecham, not the least of which was "is this a real offer?" She wanted answers to all the standard job stuff--what did the job involve, benefits, pay, reporting structure, would she need to relocate, how soon would she start. Mr. Meecham gave her a folder that he said contained documents that should answer all of her questions. Because of the nature of their work, BITES tried to maintain a low profile. The organization wasn't secret, but it also wasn't publicized due to the rampant skepticism associated with cryptids.

He explained that after she'd had lunch in the dining room, Hank would drive her back to her hotel. Hank would be able to give her an agent's view of the organization on the way. Mr. Meecham told her to take the following day to go through the paperwork and prepare any further questions. She would be brought back to the lodge day after tomorrow to meet with him again and give him her decision.

"Before I leave, there is one question you can answer. Are there any females in BITES? I've only seen men since I arrived."

"You would be our first female field agent though we have many women on the support staff and at the lab. In spite of our rocky beginning today, I hope that you will seriously consider our offer. We'd love you to join BITES," Mr. Meecham said as he rose to show her back to the sitting area. "By the way, there is a BLM shooting competition in Great Falls this weekend, and you are representing the Southwestern Region. We took advantage of that fact to introduce you to BITES."

Cassie's head was reeling. She was glad she'd have all evening and all day tomorrow to review this and determine what to do. She could just take some time to digest what she had learned. On the drive, back to the city, Hank said, "I have to ask about a rumor I heard at the lodge. Did you really pull a gun on Mr. Meecham today?"

"Truthfully yes, but it's not something I'm proud of."

"I want to apologize for all the cloak and dagger stuff earlier. I was under orders not to tell you what this was about. I hope you'll forgive me."

"I can't say that I fully understand why the organization couldn't take a more direct approach, but I do understand that you were following orders, so all is forgiven," Cassie said. "I'd appreciate it if you'd tell me your background and how you came to BITES. Mr. Meecham said that was OK. I'd like to know what you think of the organization and the work you do."

CHAPTER NINETEEN

"I grew up in Washington State near Seattle," Hank said, launching into an abbreviated version of his life story. "Great childhood, nice family. School wasn't my thing, so I joined the military right after graduation. I served six years in the Navy SEALs before returning home. I still didn't know what I wanted to do career wise but I was sure I wanted to work outside, so I took a job working security for a logging company. No office, just lots of time in the woods scouting new locations and visiting the company's logging camps to make sure things were secure."

"Sounds like the perfect job for someone with your background, so what happened?"

"Everything was great for a while. Then one day I took a road trip to visit a site the company was going to bid on for a logging contract. The location was pretty remote and the logistics would be challenging, but they thought they could make a profit. I went to check it out and see if there were any special security issues. The sun was just coming up when I got to the site. I parked the truck, grabbed my pack, and headed out to walk the perimeter."

Hank paused to take a drink of water and catch his breath, so Cassie interjected, "I haven't spent a great deal of time in the forest, but I'd like the chance to try it out sometime. Most of my outdoor experience is in desert locations, and I truly love it."

"I'm the opposite. I've spent lots of time in forests but none in the desert except when I was deployed," Hank replied and picked up his story again. "The trees at the site were massive. I could certainly see why the area would be of interest to a logging company.

"As I was nearing the back of the property, I came across a small stream. It was a pretty typical scene for the forests of Washington State. Nothing out of the ordinary at all, until I was startled by a loud howl coming from just upstream around a bend. I figured I had strayed into the territory of a bear, probably a mom with cubs, so I knew I needed to be cautious.

"I never go into the wilderness unarmed, so I pulled my gun and moved slowly back into the trees away from the stream. Then I heard the howl again. It didn't really sound like a bear, but it sounded big. I couldn't imagine what else it could be. I was curious and had to find out what it was so I could document it in my report on the risks of the area. I moved cautiously toward the sound, staying as quiet as possible, moving from tree to tree. When I could see the bend in the stream, I could also see the creature that was raising the ruckus. It was large, maybe eight feet tall and covered with reddish brown hair. It stood upright and had very long arms that ended in hands with five fingers."

"Oh my God," Cassie said. "You're telling me you saw Bigfoot."

"That or some close relative," Hank said. "I had never been a believer, but I sure converted in a hurry that day. I had a camera along to photograph any issues with the site, so I got a couple of pretty clear pictures before the creature looked directly at me. I knew I needed to get back to my truck in a hurry. I felt sure I couldn't out run it, so I settled for backing slowly and quietly away keeping my eyes on the animal the whole time. It howled once more, but I guess I reached a point that it considered far enough away, and it turned and headed into the forest in the opposite direction."

"Did you report it?"

"I spent the entire drive home considering all the possible options, but I couldn't see anyway not to include it in my report to the logging company. I thought this was sufficient reason not to log the site, but the company didn't agree. They didn't take my report seriously. They fired me on the spot."

"So how did you end up at BITES?"

"I spent the week after the encounter going over it again and again, but I knew what I had seen. I drove back out to the site two more times, but never spotted the creature again. I decided the public had a right to know, and I had proof. I went to the media. Big mistake. They published my pictures and story, but every nutcase in the northwest came out of the woodwork to comment. Whether they were supporters or not, they had something to say and none of it helped me. It really was the proverbial no-win situation. A few days after the newspaper story, I received an email about a job opportunity in Montana. The interview was with Meecham, and the rest is history, as they say."

"So did you join BITES on the spot, or did you need some time to decide?"

"It took me a couple of weeks to accept the offer," Hank admitted. "I suspect you may have experienced this too, but as much as it pisses you off that people think you're crazy because of what you say you saw, when you find a group of people who believe you, that's almost harder to accept. I accepted the fact that I had seen Bigfoot. Over the years lots of people have. But the folks involved with BITES were accepting not only the existence of Bigfoot, Nessie, and all the other strange creatures there had been legends about, but they believed there were other creatures out there we hadn't even heard of. I suspect that's a bit hard for any rational human being to come to terms with."

"I understand perfectly," Cassie agreed. "I'm feeling a lot of what you describe. How do you like the work you do with BITES?"

"It's been great. The organization is well run, the assignments are interesting, and the fieldwork is exciting. I can't imagine what I'd be doing if Mr. Meecham hadn't contacted me, but I sure am glad he did."

"Thanks for sharing your story with me. I've got a lot to consider," Cassie said.

They finished the drive in silence. Hank helped unload Cassie's gear when they reached the hotel. "I'll be back to pick you up day after tomorrow at 7:00 AM," Hank said as he left Cassie standing in the lobby with her bags at her feet.

CHAPTER TWENTY

Cassie stood in the lobby looking after Hank, not even aware she was doing so. Her mind was spinning. She considered herself a very well-grounded person, but the events of the last few months had forced her to evaluate some of her beliefs. It seemed that every time she thought things were returning to normal, something else came up that pushed her into yet another new reality. She briefly wondered if this is what going insane felt like.

"Miss, do you need some assistance?" one of the hotel employees asked, tapping her on the shoulder.

Cassie shook her head. "No. Sorry, I was just deep in thought. I'm fine. Thank you." She picked up her bags and headed for her room. It had been a long strange day. She needed a shower and several cups of very strong black coffee. Cassie always traveled with her personal coffee maker. She filled the machine with bottled water and put in her favorite Italian roast. The smell helped clear her head.

She sat down at the desk in her room with her coffee in hand and read through the paperwork Mr. Meecham had provided. Accepting the offer would nearly double her BLM salary and would be hard to turn down, but Cassie was happy with her life and just starting to build her career. She wanted to make sure she only made the change if it was the best overall decision for her. She made notes as she reviewed the information and made a list of questions to ask Mr. Meecham if she decided to consider accepting the offer. By the time she had finished, her coffee had disappeared. She looked at the clock and realized she needed to get dinner.

After a quick shower, she considered ordering take-out but decided it might help clear her head if she got out of the hotel for a bit. She dressed casually in jeans and a sweater and went to the lobby. The desk clerk gave her directions to a nice steakhouse just a block from the hotel. *Perfect*, she thought, *the walk will do me good.*

The sirloin was great and the Asiago mashed potatoes to die for. While enjoying her meal, she mulled over the offer. *Should she even consider it? Was it for real? Was Mr. Meecham for real? This setup was too elaborate to be a joke.* Her thoughts were leading her in circles again. She hated that.

By the time she got back to her hotel, she had formulated an approach to help her reach a decision. She always functioned better with a plan, even one likely to change. There were three people in her life she could turn to for advice on something like this: Her parents and Bob. She decided to give Bob a call first to get his take on her job situation. She made another cup of coffee and dialed Bob's cell phone.

"Hi, Bob. It's Cassie. How are things in Cruces?" she asked.

"Hi, Cassie. I'm surprised you can spare a minute to give us a thought. How's the competition going?"

"It's been interesting that's for sure. Do you have a few minutes to talk?"

"You know I always have time for you. Well, unless I'm hot on the trail of a giant bird. But then you'd probably be with me anyway. There hasn't been any excitement here since you left, thank God."

Cassie told Bob about BITES and her job offer, trying to be as brief as possible. She asked for his advice. He told her that he'd hate to lose her as a partner, but she had to make the best decision for her. He knew finding the Thunderbird had affected her deeply. "Cassie, if there is an organization out there protecting the rest of us from strange creatures, we will all sleep better at night knowing you're part of it."

"Could this actually be real?" Cassie asked.

"I'll admit, if we were having this conversation a few months ago, we'd probably be making fun of BITES, but since we found the Thunderbird, we both look at things differently. This doesn't sound like the kind of thing someone would make up. Why would they? What would be the point?"

"I can't imagine. It's just a lot to wrap my head around," Cassie admitted.

"You'll make the right decision. Call me back if you need to talk. A good night's sleep might help you to figure out what you want to do."

CHAPTER TWENTY-ONE

Happy to have an entire day to come to a decision about what she wanted to do, Cassie slept better than expected. Unlike most people, Cassie thrived on change. Just the thought of a new job with new people, maybe in a different location... She stopped mid-thought and added location to her list of questions for Mr. Meecham. Nothing in the paperwork she'd received had mentioned where the job was located. The idea of a fresh start was appealing.

She brewed a cup of coffee and sipped it while catching up on email. She received the competition schedule showing it started the next afternoon. She looked at the names of the competitors but didn't recognize anyone. Her coworkers emailed wishing her good luck, and there was a message from her Mom. She made some notes of her competition times and jumped in the shower.

After breakfast, she returned to her room and reviewed some of the documentation Mr. Meecham had provided again to see if she had missed something that told her where she'd be living if she accepted the offer. She didn't know if the field agents all resided in Montana or not. She didn't really think it would affect her decision, but she would definitely need to find out. She made two lists. One listed the pros of accepting the job, and the other the cons. When she had listed all the obvious things, she was surprised that the pros won hands down.

Cassie took some time to sit and think about how she would explain all this to her parents. She'd told them about finding the Thunderbird and had sent them pictures. They saw it as a great accomplishment and were really irritated with those who acted as though it wasn't real. Of course, when news of the hikers being killed got out, they were concerned about her safety, but they knew she could take care of herself.

Cassie emailed her Mom and asked her to call at lunchtime. After a short walk around the hotel grounds, she made a cup of coffee and waited for the phone to ring.

"Hi, Cass, what's up?" her Mom asked.

"Hi, Mom, I have a decision to make, and I need some advice. I'd like to get your input and Dad's. I didn't want to wait until you were home from work to call. I need an answer by tomorrow morning, and I wanted to give you some time to consider the information. I figured I could explain it to you, then you can update Dad, and both of you can give me a call back tonight."

"Sounds like a plan," her Mom said. "I'm intrigued. What's this all about?"

Cassie explained the job offer from BITES leaving out the cloak and dagger approach used to get her to Montana early. Her parents had never seriously believed in the existence of cryptids, but they were the most open-minded people she knew, and when she told them about the Thunderbird, they never questioned her sanity. Her Mom was proud of her for being offered such an important and well-paying position. Cassie explained that it was such a unique situation, she wanted their input on her decision. This wasn't like considering a job as a park ranger with the NPS instead of the BLM. This was an entirely different ball game. Her Mom asked some questions she hadn't thought of, so Cassie added those to her list.

"Thanks, Mom. I'd like you to get Dad up to speed and call me when you're both ready to tell me whether you would vote that I accept the offer or not."

"OK, Cass. I'll call Dad now and fill him in. We'll think about it this afternoon and share our wisdom with you tonight. Love you," her Mom said as she ended the call.

Well, that was that. Cassie felt like she had reviewed the information, thought it through, listed her questions, and now all she had to do was reach a decision. At this point, she was leaning toward accepting, but she'd wait to see how her parents voted when they called in a few hours. Cassie got a recommendation for lunch from the front desk and walked a few blocks to a kitschy 1950's style diner. The food was good and the atmosphere light. After she finished her meal, she ordered a chocolate milkshake to go and headed back to the hotel. She decided that the one thing she hadn't done was surf the web to see what she could learn about BITES, Mr. Meecham, Hank, or cryptids.

Cassie booted up her PC and settled in to sip her shake and investigate. After an hour of searching, she had to concede that BITES was doing a good job of keeping a low profile. They had a webpage with a vague description of what they did, and Cassie found no other information about the organization. That was amazing these days.

She found a bit of info on Mr. Meecham, but it was old. She suspected it might be from before his involvement with BITES. Info on Hank was her biggest score. The story about his Bigfoot sighting along with the photographs was on a Bigfoot related website. The pictures looked pretty convincing to her. These weren't the typical blurry pics of something peeking out from behind thick vegetation so that you might get a hint of size or color but that's really about it. These were photos of some type of very large creature.

There was a lot of info on cryptids, mostly the major ones everyone had heard of....Bigfoot, Nessie, Chupacabra, and some Cassie was much less familiar with like the Mothman and Champ. At first glance, most of the information seemed pretty unbelievable, but then again, Cassie thought, *if I were looking at photos of the Thunderbird and reading my story, I probably wouldn't believe that either.* That was one of the facets of all this that was so hard to come to grips with.

It might seem strange, but Cassie had never thought of the Thunderbird as a cryptid. She hadn't put it in the same category as Bigfoot even though she knew there were legends about Thunderbirds and reported sightings.

Absorbed in her internet research, Cassie didn't realize what time it was until her parents called. They were supportive as always. They told her that she should do what she wanted to do, and they would support her regardless of her choice. While she appreciated that, she didn't intend to let them off the hook that easily this time. "I know all that and appreciate it, but I want you each to tell me whether or not you think I should accept the position." She was surprised that both of them said she should take the job at BITES.

"Tell me why."

"Honey, you've been affected by finding the Thunderbird. You now know that there may be creatures out there we never knew existed. We know you. You'll never be able to let this go. So either it's your job or your hobby, but the job seems safer to us," her mom explained.

"Well then, I'll probably accept unless the answers to some of my questions are a problem. I'll call you tomorrow night after I've had my meeting with Mr. Meecham and made my final decision."

Cassie's mind was made-up. It was time to stop thinking about "if" and starting planning the transition. Of course, she really couldn't do much of that until after she spoke with Mr. Meecham, but at least she could give her brain a rest from the decision-making. She was tired of thinking, and she knew that not only did she have to meet with Mr. Meecham tomorrow, but it was also the start of the competition. She needed to relax, so she took a taxi to the local mall where she grabbed dinner and watched a movie.

CHAPTER TWENTY-TWO

Cassie slept soundly which she took as a sign she'd made the right decision. She dressed in her beige BLM shirt and forest green uniform pants for the competition. After breakfast, she returned to her room to grab her gear and brew a cup of coffee to take with her. When Hank arrived, she was waiting in the lobby. He helped her load her gear into the SUV, and they headed for the hills, literally.

Once they were on the road, Hank asked, "So, did you reach a decision about joining BITES?"

"I have a few more questions for Mr. Meecham, but assuming the answers are acceptable, then yes, I've decided to accept the offer," Cassie replied.

"That's great news. You'll be a great addition to the team. I think you'll enjoy the work. Let me be the first to say, welcome aboard."

"Thanks. There are a couple of questions you might be able to shed some light on. Do all BITES agents live in this area or are there teams in other places? Mr. Meecham didn't tell me where I'd need to live for the job. I'm not sure I care, but I will need to know."

"Well, I'm not sure exactly what Mr. Meecham has in mind for you, but we do have agents living throughout the US, the majority of the support staff and a few of the field agents live here in Montana," Hank responded.

"I'll have to ask him for the details of my assignment. Mr. Meecham explained that I'd be the first female BITES field agent. Since you're a team leader, I'm wondering how you feel your team would react to having a women as a team mate?"

"I guess I never really thought about it. I never stopped to wonder why we don't have any female field agents. The work is dangerous and not something that would appeal to most women, but these days, it does seem odd that we don't have any female field agents. I don't think my team would have any issues with it, but it will be a change. There are things to consider like sleeping arrangements in the field and that kind of thing. We normally carry as little gear as possible into the field if we're backpacking, so a normal BITES team would have two tents with two team members sharing each one. I assume they don't plan to change that to accommodate a woman. I hope we're all adult enough to handle it. There might be some BITES agents who will find it uncomfortable to be in the field with a woman."

"I appreciate your honesty, Hank. I want to make sure I'm not getting into a situation where I'm the 'token female' to meet some equality criteria or something."

"I'd mention your concern to Mr. Meecham. I've found that he's usually a pretty straight-forward guy."

During the remainder of the drive, Hank asked Cassie questions about her shooting competitions and about the Thunderbird. It was a pleasant ride, but Cassie was anxious to get to the lodge, finalize her decision, and shift her brain into competitor mode.

She waited in the sitting area until Mr. Meecham was available. As she entered his office, he came around the desk to shake her hand. "Well, Ms. Carter, have you reached a decision about our offer?"

"I believe so, but I do have a few more questions before I'm ready to sign on the dotted line."

Over the next hour, he answered all of Cassie's questions. For now, she could live anywhere in the southwestern US. That would be her area of focus, and as long as she had reasonable airport access, she would not be required to relocate. BITES team members were assigned specific areas of responsibility, but during major operations, agents could be called in from any location. Because of Cassie's knowledge of the desert and her current home, she would be involved in all investigations in her home area. She would also be the BITES expert on anything insect related due to her entomology degree. There were a few cryptids in that category, and Mr. Meecham expected there would be more found in the future.

When Cassie voiced her concerns about being the "token" female, Mr. Meecham explained. "I assure you, Cassie, BITES would have been happy to have a female agent sooner, but I'm sure you can understand that there are few women who would meet all our requirements and be interested in this type of work. We certainly hope to add more women in the future, but that requires us to find the right candidates. We hope that having you on the team will help with that. While I can assure you, you will be treated as any other field agent, I will admit that there may come a time when we ask you to speak to other female candidates or something of that nature."

"I understand and would certainly be happy to share my BITES experience honestly with other women."

After her competition was over, Cassie would go home to Las Cruces and turn in her notice to the BLM. She would start work for BITES in four weeks. She'd come back to the lodge for a month of training covering investigative techniques, security protocols, weapons handling, and field operations. Cassie signed the required documents and received some further paperwork to review before the start of her training. She packed away all her job related information and ate lunch in the dining room before Hank drove her to the competition.

X X X

The Shoot Out was only for BLM rangers, so it was fairly small with no separate division for women. Cassie was the only female competitor. There were several creative and fun challenges. It was great to meet so many new people. While there was some serious shooting involved, this competition was much more fun than most. Cassie had to admit, that she was less interested in the competition now than she might have been if she didn't know she would soon be leaving the BLM. She enjoyed meeting everyone, but it was unlikely she'd cross paths with any of them again. She found it difficult to engage in conversations centered on the BLM when she was preparing to close that chapter in her life. At the end of the first day of competition, a shuttle returned all the competitors to their hotels.

Once the other rangers realized she was the one who discovered the Thunderbird that was all they wanted to talk about with her. They all had tons of questions, and it was a great diversion for Cassie. She enjoyed herself and focused on the competition. She placed second behind a ranger from Maine.

When the competition ended, Cassie headed back to New Mexico pleased with her results and happy to begin her transition to BITES.

CHAPTER TWENTY-THREE

When she arrived back in Las Cruces, Cassie spent the rest of her day unpacking, catching up on laundry, and writing her resignation letter for Cory. She called Bob and told him she had accepted the job offer. He congratulated her and said it was great that she'd be staying in Las Cruces, so they could still get together frequently. The FWS team studying the Thunderbird had gathered a huge amount of information from the nesting site where Marina was found. They were adding more data to the knowledge of the species daily.

After dinner, Cassie took a walk over to the Lewis' to find out how Trevor was doing. He wasn't home but Mrs. Lewis thanked Cassie for coming by to check on him. His mom said he was doing well though the death of his friend hit him hard. She told Cassie that she'd heard that Marina was recovering, but her parents thought the psychological scars would take a lot longer to heal than the physical ones. Cassie asked Mrs. Lewis to tell Trevor she stopped by.

In some ways, Cassie saw it as tying up loose ends. She figured it was just part of the process of moving on to the next chapter in her life. Thinking back over the last few months, she found it hard to believe all that had happened. She had been abducted at gunpoint, discovered a new species, broken up with her longtime boyfriend, and now accepted a new job. She thrived on change, but this had been a lot, even for her.

X X X

At the morning "stand up" meeting, Cory told everyone about Cassie's finish in the shooting competition and everyone applauded. After the meeting broke up, she asked to speak with

Cory. She explained that she had accepted another job and would be leaving the BLM. She turned in her official resignation letter and negotiated with Cory to wrap things up in two to three weeks, leaving her enough downtime to visit her folks in Texas for a few days before heading to Montana to start her training. The day in the office was quiet as Cassie caught up on emails and paperwork. The FWS research team emailed requesting another interview with her. She couldn't imagine why. She had already told them everything she knew about the Thunderbird.

X X X

Still catching up from the trip and the excitement, she planned to just relax at home in the evening. When she checked her email, there was a message from Hank which surprised her. It was very casual, just hoping she had a good trip back and looking forward to seeing her when she returned to Montana for training in a few weeks. She didn't know if it was a gesture of friendship or an assignment he'd been given, but she appreciated it either way. One of her biggest concerns about the way BITES worked was that she wouldn't be seeing the same people five days a week. She didn't really consider herself a people person, but she liked to have a few close friends. By staying in Las Cruces, she could maintain her existing friendships while getting to know her fellow BITES employees. It was a win-win for her.

X X X

At work the next day, Cory announced Cassie's departure during the morning stand-up. Everyone voiced their sadness at her leaving but congratulated her on her new position. Folks wanted details on where she was going. She wasn't sure how to answer those questions, so she told them she was joining another federal agency, but she couldn't say which one. They all accepted that, but interpreted it to mean FBI or CIA or maybe even NSA, but they didn't push for more information after that, which was good.

Cassie agreed to meet with the FWS researchers at their campsite in the afternoon. It was a quiet patrol day, so she had time to update Bob on the details of her trip. He was surprised by the secrecy surrounding BITES at first, but then realized that it was because of the stigma attached to any mention of cryptids, which he and Cassie had experienced firsthand.

The researchers asked Bob and Cassie some of the same questions they'd already answered, but did have some new ones. Their main concern seemed to focus on whether or not there could be more than one Thunderbird in the area. The reason for their concern stemmed from the fact that a close inspection of the nest where they had found Marina had turned up pieces of egg shell. They tested the shells and learned they were not the eggs of some other creature that the bird had carried to the nest and eaten. They were Thunderbird egg shells that had hatched and most likely, produced more Thunderbirds.

Cassie and Bob were shocked. "I never thought about where the bird came from or if it was the only one," Cassie admitted on the drive to the office.

"Me either," Bob said. "I guess it makes sense that it didn't just appear out of thin air, but I sure don't like the idea that there could be more of those things running around out here."

X X X

At home that night, Cassie started going through the dossiers on her teammates. Her team consisted of four people--one team leader and three field agents. Jim Lansing, the team leader, had been with BITES for several years. He was a retired detective in his fifties who lived in Las Vegas. One of his special skills listed was interrogating witnesses. Cassie could understand how that would be helpful when investigating cryptid sightings.

Her fellow field agents were Garrett Acton from Colorado and Pat Murphy from Arizona. Garrett, an academic who had written books on cryptids, raced ATVs and listed his special skill as planning and tactics. Pat was originally from Ireland. On a holiday to Scotland as a teenager, he took what were widely considered to be the most indisputable photographs of Nessie. Not surprisingly, he listed his special skill as photography. It sounded like an interesting group. Cassie looked forward to meeting them.

She was a little surprised by their backgrounds. She assumed, because of the amount of wilderness work involved, that most field agents would be real outdoorsmen like Hank, but on paper, her teammates seemed like they might be more comfortable in an office than out in the wild. It would be interesting to meet them in person and see if her assessment had been correct. The team statistics indicated they had investigated twenty-six cryptid reports resulting in one kill. She'd have to ask Jim for the details.

When Jim called later that week, Cassie immediately found him likeable. She couldn't really assess how he'd function as a team leader but he seemed like a reasonable, competent person.

She told him about herself, and he did likewise. He asked many questions about the Thunderbird situation, and she agreed to email him photos. He gave her a brief overview of each of her new teammates and the team's history in the field. Jim told her that BITES had been monitoring the situation with her giant bird and if it escalated, the team might be called in. He asked lots of questions about her shooting abilities and her background in entomology. All in all, it was a pleasant conversation, and so far, Cassie felt she'd be able to work well with Jim.

CHAPTER TWENTY-FOUR

On one of Bob and Cassie's last patrol days together, they were checking out a remote area on the far southeastern edge of the Organ Mountains. This part of the desert had no publicized trails and abutted White Sands Missile Range, so it attracted little public attention. Because of that, the rangers only patrolled the area once every three weeks or so depending on available manpower. They drove in as far as possible, parked, and put on their packs. It was a nice day for a hike, the unseasonably warm spring weather had returned to something more normal for this time of year. Hiking in the desert and calling it work just seemed wrong to Cassie. She loved it and enjoyed talking with Bob while they explored. A large part of the job of patrolling was keeping your eyes open and being aware of your surroundings. Cassie really felt sorry for the rangers who didn't appreciate how special this part of the job was. She hoped her BITES investigations would provide similar opportunities though she doubted it would be part of her daily routine.

They scrambled up a ridge and sat at the top eating their lunch and taking in the surrounding desert. Bob put down his sandwich and picked up the binoculars. Cassie stopped eating to see what had caught Bob's attention. "Thunderbird sighting on the far ridge," Bob said, pointing to a ridge somewhat north and east of where they were sitting.

"Wow, I think I see more than one," Cassie said. "Are you seeing that too?"

Bob passed the binoculars to Cassie. "With these I'm pretty sure there are three."

"You're right. We'd better note the GPS coordinates and report this to the FWS team."

They worked their way a bit closer to the birds and Cassie took out her camera and got some shots of the group. Eventually, the three birds climbed up over the ridge and disappeared from view. Cassie wondered aloud, "I can't figure out why all of a sudden we're seeing these things that had never been seen before. Do you think something is causing them to move into new areas?"

Bob thought about it, "The only thing I could see is if their food source is disappearing. That might force them to expand their territory. Could be the drought."

X X X

Back at home that night, Cassie printed up the photos and emailed them to her FWS contact as well as to Jim and Bob.

Later that week, while out on patrol, they got a call to assist in the search for a missing child that had disappeared while playing in her yard that backed up to BLM land. Cassie prayed this would have nothing to do with the Thunderbirds. Just before calling off the search for the night the little girl was discovered scared but fine. She had climbed up some rocks and fallen into a crack. Her foot was stuck, and she couldn't get out. The searchers were able to move the rocks and pull her leg out without injury.

Even though this incident had nothing to do with the Thunderbirds, the media saw it as an excuse to resurrect all the terrible things that had happened in the desert that year, and that included rehashing the deaths associated with the bird. It brought the issue back into the forefront for the public. The internet and local media were once again filled with comments and op-ed pieces about how dangerous these birds were.

Unfortunately, in trying to find a new angle on old news, a reporter talked with one of the FWS researchers who confirmed that multiple Thunderbirds had been spotted. This was just the hook needed to raise the issue to the boiling point again. The stories made it sound as though you couldn't set foot in the desert east of Las Cruces without seeing a Thunderbird. Cassie and Bob knew that wasn't true, but lots of folks believed it.

The anger toward Bob and Cassie because they had found the birds started up again. Cassie was really getting tired of it. She knew that there were many deadly creatures in the desert, but people never worried about it until there was a story in the media. It was the same way with sharks. Every time a person went into the ocean it was possible that they would be attacked by a shark, but no one made an issue of it until someone was attacked. Then, for a few weeks, there would be a public outcry. Over time the interest level would subside, replaced by some other event until the next attack.

Of course, there was the other side of the coin. There were the "environmental whackos" as Bob liked to call them, who wanted to set up a Thunderbird preserve to protect the birds and people's rights be damned.

Both sides were extremists and Cassie wanted no part of either. She just wanted to do her job, live her life, and be left alone.

CHAPTER TWENTY-FIVE

Cassie had a goodbye lunch with her colleagues at the BLM. She really appreciated the Amazon gift card she received. It wasn't so much the card itself that impressed her as the fact that they knew her well enough to choose something she'd like. Cassie didn't like trinkets. She liked functional things and was happy to get a really useful item instead of a cute gecko statue or a stuffed bear. She suspected Bob was behind the choice. She appreciated all the warm wishes for her continued success. She cleared out her desk and locker before heading home, a little sad to close the book on this chapter of her life. She'd enjoyed her time with the BLM, but she was ready to move on.

Cassie enjoyed a day off to catch up on reading the information from BITES that she needed to study before starting her training. It was nice to have a break from her old BLM routine to allow her to shift gears into her new job. She couldn't believe in less than two weeks she'd be headed back to Montana. Hank emailed almost every day. They had become good friends which made it even more exciting to look forward to her time at the lodge.

Cassie had a great visit with her folks, as always. They lived in a small town called Mars, Texas near Waco. The ten hour drive was a little too long unless someone else shared the trip, so Cassie flew. They laughed, shopped, ate, and enjoyed each other's company. Cassie loved spending time with her mom and dad, but she was anxious to head home and get ready for her training. She also needed to spend some time at the shooting range. With so much going on in her life lately, she hadn't found time to focus on preparations for her upcoming competitions.

X X X

Back in Las Cruces, Cassie concentrated on studying her BITES material and hitting the range. She scheduled a dinner with Bob and corresponded regularly with her new team mates and Hank. She enjoyed spending several hours at the range each day to break up her study sessions. Over dinner, she learned Bob had a new partner, Jeremy, who he liked well enough, but it was a change. He doubted he'd ever be as close to another partner as he'd been to Cassie. She told Bob she'd be out of town for four weeks for training. He'd check on her condo from time to time, and she asked him to email or call her if anything new developed with the Thunderbirds.

X X X

It surprised Cassie when Hank called one evening. He asked if she'd like to come to Montana early and spend the weekend sightseeing before starting her training. He knew she hadn't had the opportunity to see much when she was in the area for her interview and competition. During training, she'd be staying at the lodge, so she figured her new salary allowed her to splurge on a couple of nights in a hotel to enjoy seeing more of Montana. She loved exploring new areas and saw very little during her last visit.

The FWS researchers emailed with more questions which she answered as well as she could. All of her new teammates sent her good luck wishes for her training.

Hank offered to pick her up at the airport, so she took a later flight that would get her into Montana around 7:00 PM Friday night. Usually when she traveled she booked the first flight out in the morning. With the El Paso airport being an hour's drive from Cruces, it meant getting up in the middle of the night. She really enjoyed having a quiet morning with her coffee before closing up her condo and heading out.

X X X

The flight was uneventful, which was always a good thing, and Hank greeted her when she got to baggage claim. As always, he was wearing a BITES polo and khakis. She'd have to find out if that was the required uniform or just his personal preference. After a warm hug, he helped her with her luggage. This time he drove his own truck, a 4WD F150 with a cap. They loaded Cassie's gear in the back and headed out of the airport. Now that she was part of BITES, Hank freely shared stories of his investigations. Over dinner, she learned a lot about BITES, cryptids, and perhaps most importantly, about Hank.

Cassie had always been very driven and goal-oriented. When she was in school, she was totally focused on her studies, and then her shooting became her major emphasis. Now her career had taken top priority. She could sometimes be a little slow to pick up on interpersonal signals, but by the end of dinner, she was wondering if perhaps Hank wanted to be more than friends. She found she rather liked the idea. They had really grown close through their emails. Seeing him again, she realized that she found him attractive in that dark brooding way that so many women seemed drawn to. But, she reminded herself, she needed to focus on her new job and her training. She'd see how this thing with Hank developed. She'd misread things before. By the time they finished desert, Cassie was yawning. A ten-mile hike didn't tire her out as much as two hours on a plane.

"Looks like I need to get you into bed," Hank said. They both laughed at the unintended innuendo. "Let's get the check and get out of here."

"Thanks, Hank. I assure you it's not the company. Travel just wipes me out."

Hank drove to Cassie's hotel and carried her bags to her room. They ended the night with a hug and plans to meet in the lobby in the morning.

CHAPTER TWENTY-SIX

Cassie had a great weekend. It was fun from start to finish. Excited and maybe a little nervous about starting her BITES training on Monday, the next two days she was going to enjoy herself and try not to think about the challenges that might be looming on the horizon.

Hank told her to dress for the outdoors, so she wore her favorite cargo pants, T-shirt, and flannel over shirt. She packed a sweatshirt and sweater in her backpack along with a hat and gloves. In a separate bag were her hiking boots, canteen, and binoculars. She didn't know where they were going, so she tried to take everything she might need.

Cassie took along a fresh brewed cup of her favorite coffee and was waiting in the lobby when Hank arrived. He loaded her stuff in the truck, and they headed off. "It seems like you always have a cup of coffee in your hand when I pick you up. Does the hotel have a special roast they use?" Hank asked.

Cassie laughed, "Oh no, I'm serious about my coffee. I brought this from home. I drink it black and really enjoy a flavorful Italian roast, so I never travel without my coffee-maker and my own coffee."

"Wow, you are serious about your coffee," Hank said. "I'll have to try it sometime."

"I think that can be arranged."

They headed to Glacier National Park to do some hiking. Stopping at a truck stop on the edge of the city, they ate a lumberjack breakfast.

Cassie always enjoyed being in the wilderness, but the forests of Montana were quite a switch from her usual desert haunts. She appreciated how beautiful it was but found it somewhat claustrophobic. The tree cover was so thick that traveling on the mountain roads was like being in one long continuous tunnel.

When they got back into town that evening, they enjoyed a nice dinner before Hank dropped her off at the hotel. He promised the next day would be more driving and less hiking. They planned to finish up early so Cassie would be well rested to start her training on Monday.

By Saturday night, she was tired and more relaxed than she'd felt in a long time. It surprised her that she had enjoyed the mountains and forests, though if she was being honest with herself, she wasn't sure which she had found more appealing-- Hank or the environment. He was a great tour guide, and she really enjoyed his company.

On Sunday morning, Cassie waited in the lobby for Hank with two cups of coffee.

"Not bad," Hank said as he sipped the rich dark coffee. "I can see why you like this so much. I have to admit though, I'm going add some cream and sugar to mine." He used the beverage counter the hotel had set up to fix up his coffee before they headed out. It was another beautiful day. The extra days in Montana had definitely been a good transition.

After breakfast, they went for a scenic drive into the mountains. Hank had brought along a picnic lunch which they enjoyed beside a picture perfect mountain lake. They got to know each other better, talking about their childhoods and families. They hiked around the lake and then headed back to town.

Hank walked Cassie to her room and she said good-bye with a kiss on the cheek. She ordered pizza delivery so she could just crash and prepare for tomorrow. She caught up on emails, called her folks, and did a little more studying before calling it a night.

CHAPTER TWENTY-SEVEN

Cassie was waiting in the lobby when Hank arrived. She had already checked out. She held two cups of coffee, one with cream and sugar for Hank. He took the cup she offered and helped load her luggage into his truck. The sun started to peek over the mountains as they drove north out of the city. As the miles rolled by, her thoughts wandered back to the first time she had made this drive with Hank a little over a month ago. She had been so busy and so much had happened during the ensuing weeks that she felt like it happened a long time ago.

She remembered how she had believed she was only here for a competition. She didn't even know that BITES existed back then and she had been so nervous because of all the secrecy. Now she was calm, relaxed, and excited to go to work for BITES. Thinking about it brought a smile to her lips. Six months ago she was an avowed skeptic who didn't believe in cryptids. *Wow, things sure can change dramatically in a very short time*, she thought to herself.

"You're awfully quiet this morning," Hank said. "Is everything all right?"

"Every thing's great," Cassie answered. "Just thinking about all the changes in my life these past few months and remembering how much of a hard time I gave you on my first visit. After that trip, if anyone had asked me if you and I would become friends, I'm sure I would have laughed at the idea."

"You certainly didn't make my job easy," Hank said.

At the lodge, Hank introduced her to the manager who showed her to her room in the west wing. She unpacked and was waiting in the sitting area when Mr. Meecham came to greet her.

The first hour was spent going over additional paperwork and filling-out forms. Cassie got her training schedule and only then realized that the training was just for her. There were no other field agents going through training with her. Much of the first week would be spent with various members of the support staff learning what resources would be at her disposal and how to access them. Everyone she met was helpful and friendly.

Sometimes she ran into Hank around the lodge and some days they ate lunch together. He introduced her to folks she didn't know and answered questions that came up during her training.

Her room at the lodge was wonderful. Like the common areas, it was decorated in lodge decor with flannel sheets on the bed, lots of quilts, and throw rugs on the wide pine hardwood floors. She had a private bath and a window that looked out over the lake at the back of the lodge. It was a beautiful and peaceful environment, very conducive to learning.

Cassie found out she would have weekends off to relax, so she and Hank made plans to spend more time together.

After the first few days, she learned that the lodge had its own chef. Chef Loren would make anything you requested, and he didn't just make it, he seemed to make it the best you'd ever tasted. She enjoyed massive breakfasts and delicious light lunches. Dinner ranged from beef stew, to steak, to gourmet pizza. Whatever the menu, it was all wonderful and followed by heavenly desert options like chocolate mousse or warm apple compote. Cassie felt as though she was staying in a four star resort.

Friday of Cassie's first week was spent learning research methods and how to utilize the BITES database of cryptid data. The database contained data on every cryptid and every cryptid sighting reported in the US. The research team gathered new reports, cataloged them in the database, and did everything possible to determine if they were true or not. Once a report was investigated, if it appeared to be factual, a copy would be sent to the field team leader for the region where the sighting occurred. The team leader would do further investigation and, if appropriate, activate his team to pursue the incident in person. Cassie knew she could spend hours learning about all the cryptids in the database, but the training was to teach her how to find what she needed, so Angela, her trainer for the database, suggested she spend the afternoon researching the information on the Thunderbirds.

Angela explained that since Cassie was now a member of BITES, it provided them a unique opportunity to have her review the data and their assessment of it. She could provide them with feedback on how to better interpret the reports. Cassie got that surreal feeling again as she read reports about herself and the birds. She was surprised they had information on the Thunderbirds that even she had not seen before. At the end of the day, she met with Angela and gave her assessment of the information they had gathered and where they might have missed something or misinterpreted. For the most part, the data they had on the Thunderbirds was thorough and accurate. The fact that Cassie had joined BITES was noted in the file.

She spent a quiet Friday night at the lodge, making notes from her first week of training and reviewing the schedule for the upcoming week.

X X X

Hank picked her up on Saturday, and they headed out for a hike near the lodge after enjoying one of Chef's massive breakfasts.

Hank had Chef pack a picnic lunch for them, and they enjoyed a great day in the woods. Another perfect day ended with one of Chef Loren's fabulous dinners at the lodge. With only the two of them, it was like having a four star restaurant all to yourself.

On Sunday morning, Hank picked Cassie up and they headed to town. She needed to resupply her room. They decided it would be nice to take a break from the lodge since they spent so much time there during the week. They ate breakfast at the truck stop on the edge of the city, and Hank drove around showing Cassie the sights. They spent the afternoon shopping. Cassie picked up a case of bottled water to make her coffee in her room and some office supplies she needed to keep her notes and paperwork organized. They were enjoying an early dinner when Hank's phone rang.

"I have to take this, it's work," Hank said as he walked outside so as not to disturb the other diners. When he returned he explained, "My team has been activated to investigate some new Bigfoot sightings in Washington State. I'll be heading out tomorrow morning."

"Do you get called out for Bigfoot stuff often?"

"Maybe once every couple of months on average," Hank explained. "Bigfoot is the best known US Cryptid, so it gets the most reports. Of course, most of them end up being hoaxes, but we have to check out any that seem credible. Such is the life of a BITES agent."

"When you return, I hope you can fill me in on the details. I'd like to understand what an active investigation is really like," Cassie said.

"Sure thing, but from what I've read in the files, you've been experiencing pretty much the same thing since you discovered the Thunderbird. Only difference is that I'll have a team working with me. You and Bob handled things on your own until the FWS got involved."

"I guess you're right, but I still want details."

The ride back to the lodge was a little surreal for Cassie. As darkness descended, Hank regaled her with details of his closest encounters with Bigfoot. The thick forests cast deep shadows over the road. Trying to look into the trees as they drove past, she could believe there could be almost anything hiding in there. As he walked her to her room he explained, "We never know how long we'll be gone, but I'll keep in touch when I can. When I get back, we'll have dinner, and I'll give you all the details, I promise."

"I hope you get back before I finish my training. Be safe," Cassie said as she hugged him. He looked into her eyes and they shared a brief kiss. "Good night, Hank. Safe travels," she called as she closed the door to her room. As she walked past the mirror she stopped, noticing the silly smile on her face. She enjoyed Hank's company and attention. She had no idea where this was going, but she was glad to be along for the ride.

CHAPTER TWENTY-EIGHT

Week two of Cassie's training would focus on physical fitness, outdoor survival skills, and weapons training. Cassie wasn't too concerned about any of those areas and looked forward to some physical activity after all the time in front of the computer during the first week.

The fitness trainer explained that BITES didn't expect its agents would be running down cryptids literally, but it wanted to give them an easy fitness routine that they could incorporate into their daily lives so they stayed in good shape and could "run for their lives" if necessary. Cassie hoped he meant the last comment to be a joke.

Training began with thirty minutes of exercises and stretching and ended with a two-mile run. Cassie could hike in the desert for hours, but she didn't do a lot of running and at this altitude, it was pushing her limits, but she felt good when she made it back to the lodge.

She showered, changed, and met her outdoor skills instructor. He asked her to describe her outdoor experiences. After their talk, he could see she was well versed in desert survival skills and there was no need to spend any time on that. Mountains, forests, and cold weather survival techniques are what they would focus on for the week. Although Cassie was assigned to the Southwest region, she could be called to join an investigation anywhere in the US, so she needed to be prepared for the challenges of other environments. Regional team leaders would normally be from the area where the operation took place. so the primary lesson was to follow the lead of those who knew the environment better than you. Cassie understood that every environment posed its own special hurdles to survival. She enjoyed learning about areas she didn't know much about.

After lunch, Cassie met her weapons trainer. Having read her file, he expected shooting wouldn't be much of a challenge for her. The BITES arsenal included pistols, rifles, tranquilizer guns of various sizes, net guns, and crossbows. Shooting came naturally to Cassie, so she really only needed to learn the mechanics of each weapon. Her instructor was very impressed with her skills.

That night after dinner, Cassie got a call from Hank. His team had completed interviewing those involved in the report and was heading into the woods to search for the creature or at least hard evidence of its existence. He would be out of communication until they returned to civilization.

Cassie was happy to hear from Hank and had to admit she missed seeing him around the lodge, but it did give her time to concentrate on her training. The rest of the week went well. On Thursday, her weapons instructor said she was finished with that part of training. He made notes in her file that she should be considered to serve as a firearms instructor for other agents if she was available. He recommended she be involved in field testing any weapons BITES was considering adding to their arsenal. He told her the scores on her final shooting test were the highest recorded by any BITES agent. It was good to know that she was doing well. He told her he'd be cheering her on during the US championships and expected to see her on Top Shot someday.

Cassie hadn't heard from Hank and that bothered her a bit. She wondered if he was back in Montana or still in the field. She had thought they were really building a connection but maybe she'd been wrong about that. She realized that this might just be a typical circumstance for a field agent. When they last spoke, he had said he would be out of contact, but she had thought it would only be for two or three days. That would be tough in a normal relationship. She always felt insecure in her relationships. She thought that would change with age and experience, but it hadn't.

She spent a quiet weekend at the lodge, catching up on reading, keeping up with her physical fitness routine, and getting in some extra shooting practice at the range. It was restful and relaxing. She wasn't sure what was on tap for the next week, but she felt ready for it.

CHAPTER TWENTY-NINE

Training week three started with testing to determine what areas Cassie might need to work on in the remaining weeks. Every day now began with a two mile run. Last thing Monday morning was a meeting with Mr. Meecham to discuss her progress thus far and talk about the schedule for the remainder of her training. He told her that her weapons test scores were the highest overall of any agent they had trained. All her other ratings were excellent as well. He asked her if she had any questions for him at this point.

"No, sir. I think things are going well, but I am curious about the remainder of my training time. The schedule is a little vague."

He explained that the remainder of her training would be spent actually working on an investigation with the research staff and doing some training drills which closely simulated what she might experience in the field. They hoped to send her out on a live field op with an experienced team if something appropriate became active before she returned home.

She was assigned research related to the latest reports about Montana's own cryptid, the Flathead Lake Monster. The monster was most often described as some type of water-based creature similar to Champ, the monster said to inhabit Lake Champlain on the Vermont-New York state line. The first reported sighting of the Flathead Lake Monster occurred in the late eighteen hundreds. A few sightings are reported each year. Flathead Lake is in northwest Montana and is the largest lake in the western US. The BITES database had lots of information on the monster. The latest sighting was by a family fishing early in the morning. There were hazy cell phone photos and the statements of the family. She wasn't sure if they had really seen the creature or not. The photographic evidence wasn't conclusive, but it was clear that they believed they had seen it.

Cassie was introduced to Jack Haney who ran the photo lab for BITES. Jack tested any photographic evidence to assess its authenticity. He explained the steps he went through to determine if a photograph or video had been tampered with or manipulated in some way. Cassie was fascinated. She did a lot of insect photography and used Photoshop to process her photos, but she was not aware of all the ways you could detect manipulation. She liked Jack immediately. He reminded her of Bob. He clearly loved his job and was excited to play a role in cryptid investigations. He complemented her on the Thunderbird pictures he had seen and told her he'd like to see some of her insect photography. She showed him her Flickr account. It was a thoroughly enjoyable afternoon.

When Cassie went to her room to relax before dinner, she found an envelope taped to her door containing a note from Mr. Meecham. "Cassie your training has gone very well. I am anxious for you to get a taste of field work, so pack a bag, and be in the sitting area tomorrow morning at 7:00 AM."

Cassie wondered why he didn't tell her where she was going. She started to think Mr. Meecham liked to keep secrets to drive his agents crazy. After dinner, she made a list of what to pack and started laying things out on the bed. Without knowing where she was headed, she had no idea what type of weather to prepare for. She assumed that field work would mean outdoors so casual clothes and hiking gear for sure. Later that night Hank called.

"Hi, Cassie, I can't wait to see you tomorrow."

"Hi, Hank. I'd love to see you to, but I'm afraid Mr. Meecham has decided to send me into the field tomorrow. He didn't tell me where I'm going or what team I'm joining. All I know is that I have to be ready to leave at 7:00 AM."

Hank laughed.

"I'm not sure why you think that's funny," Cassie said, feeling a little hurt. "My training has gone well, and Mr. Meecham wants me to get some field experience."

"I'm sorry, Cassie. I should have realized Mr. Meecham would keep you in the dark. You're coming to Washington to join my team in the field. We were wrapping up our investigation of the report that brought us here when another report came in from the same general area. We're starting the investigation of the new sighting tomorrow. Mr. Meecham called and said he'd like to have you join us to experience some field work. Of course, I told him I'd be happy to have you."

"I'm sorry. I thought you were laughing at the idea of my being in the field on a real case."

"Not at all. From what I hear, you're acing your training and everyone is very impressed with you. I'm glad to be part of your first field experience. I'll be waiting for you at the airport. Good night."

Cassie knew she was grinning again. She was pleased with herself. She was doing well and felt ready to experience field work first hand. She was happy to share that experience with a good friend like Hank.

X X X

"Hi, Cassie, I'll be driving you to the airport. Are you all set to go?" Chef Loren asked.

"I am, but I'm curious. How can you leave at breakfast time?"

"Only the regular staff is here today and my assistant can handle it. I need to get some supplies in town, so Mr. Meecham asked if I'd mind going early and dropping you off at the airport."

During the drive, Cassie and Loren got better acquainted. He was a Le Cordon Bleu trained chef and had worked in some well-known restaurants in Chicago. He liked to hunt. On a trip to Alaska a few years ago, his guide had to find a new way out of the forest due to a wildfire. During their run to escape the fire, they encountered a large, white wolf-like creature that the guide called Waheela. His group found themselves running from the fire and the creature. He wasn't sure which was more frightening. Once back home, he started investigating the Waheela, a cross between a wolf and a bear, according to Inuit legend. His research efforts brought him to the attention of Mr. Meecham who offered him the position of executive chef at the lodge. The job allowed him to do the cooking he loved, but also stay involved with the search for the Waheela. It let him be surrounded by others who believed this creature could actually exist instead of those who labeled him as nuts.

Cassie told him about her discovery of the Thunderbird and how she had experienced similar reactions from most folks. She completely understood and realized that most, if not all, of the people working for BITES had experience with cryptids and wanted to be involved in finding proof and avoiding the rampant skepticism of the general population.

"I hope you don't mind my asking, but is there something going on with you and Hank?" Loren asked.

Cassie laughed. "I'm not sure how to answer that, but I hope the correct answer is yes."

CHAPTER THIRTY

On the flight, Cassie ran through her training in her head and hoped she was ready for fieldwork. In some ways, it would be easier with Hank there, but on the other side of the coin, she wanted to impress him and that was added pressure. She told herself if she was well prepared, it wouldn't matter. Time would tell.

He was waiting for her in baggage claim and greeted her with a hug and a quick kiss. "It's nice to see you, Cassie. Are you ready for this?" he asked.

Cassie was a little surprised by the greeting. She had expected him to be all business. "It's nice to see you too," Cassie responded reaching down to pick up her duffel bag off the carousel. "I think I'm as ready as I can be at this stage. I missed seeing you around the lodge."

"I've been trying to decide whether I should admit to you that I don't know which I missed more, you or the Italian roast."

Cassie punched him in the shoulder laughing, "Either way, it's all about me, so it's all good, as far as I'm concerned."

X X X

It took about three hours for them to drive to where the team had set up operations in a small motel in the town closest to the location of the reported sightings. When they stopped for lunch along the way, Hank gave Cassie an overview of his team members, Auggie Harris, Grant White, and Larry Zuck. Hank's team had been together for the past eighteen months, Zuck being the newest member. Each had their own reasons for coming to BITES, but he trusted them all and felt they were all good field agents.

X X X

Cassie checked into her room and went to meet the team members gathered in Hank's room. There was a topo map pinned to the wall and photos tacked up everywhere. To bring Cassie up to speed, they reviewed what they learned from the investigation of the first report. Two guys out hiking came across an extremely large foot print in the mud near a creek. It was only a couple of miles from where they parked their truck, and this being Washington State, they quickly jumped to the conclusion that it must have been made by Bigfoot.

One of them stayed to guard the spot, while the other drove into town and brought back the supplies to make a cast of the print. The team had seen the cast, examined the photos taken by the hunters, and interviewed the two men involved. In addition, they interviewed acquaintances of the men to ascertain if they were likely to try to pull off a hoax.

The investigation indicated that the men were being honest in their report and believed the print was that of Bigfoot. The team spent four days in the woods in the area where the print was found, but they failed to find any further evidence of a large creature of any type. They had been preparing to close their op when a family camping in the wilderness reported a creature sighting. The location was less than twenty miles from where the print was found, so the team decided to stay and investigate the new sighting as well. Hank explained that when he called Meecham to let him know the team would be continuing the search, Mr. Meecham asked if Hank would be willing to have Cassie join the team in the field.

It was late afternoon by the time Cassie was up to speed on the case. They wrapped up by planning the activities for the following day and making assignments.

Hank took Cassie to dinner at the only real restaurant in town. She asked lots of questions about the case. She asked Hank if he thought anyone on his team would have a problem working with her in the field because she was female. They had all been polite, but something seemed off about Zuck's attitude. She didn't mention it to Hank, but she wanted to know how he thought they were going to handle the situation.

"I wouldn't have agreed to have you join the investigation if I thought any of the team would have a problem with it. But if you feel there's an issue with anyone, let me know. As team leader, it's my responsibility to deal with any interpersonal issues."

Cassie assured him she didn't expect there to be any problems.

He told her he was looking forward to working with her but didn't want it to affect their relationship. "I know we haven't known each other long, but I feel like we have a real connection. I think we're both mature enough to keep our relationship separate from our working together," he told her as they left the restaurant.

Later that night in her hotel room, Cassie laughed thinking back on it. Right after he said that, he stopped and kissed her before they got back to the hotel. She wasn't really sure that was keeping things as separate as she had expected, but they were both adults, and she trusted he knew what he was doing.

CHAPTER THIRTY-ONE

Over breakfast the next morning, they reviewed the plan and assignments for the day. Hank and Cassie would interview the Evanston family. Hank felt it was important for Cassie to experience the process from the beginning. Unless there were some extremely unusual circumstances, two BITES agents conducted each interview. This gave them different views of the information, so it wasn't just one person's assessment. While Cassie and Hank interviewed the Evanstons, Auggie, Zuck, and Grant would be interviewing friends and family of the Evanstons. This was the character reference portion of the investigation intended to determine whether or not the person making the report was a believable witness or if they might be perpetrating a hoax.

The information gathered from the interviews would help the team decide if the investigation moved on to the next stage. If it was decided that the report was not credible, then Hank would file a report and recommend the case be closed. If the information from the interviews indicated that the report was a valid account, Hank would recommend moving ahead with the field hunt.

X X X

Cassie and Hank met with Mrs. Evanston and the children at their home a few blocks from the motel where the team was staying. The son was six years old and the daughter eight. After the agents introduced themselves and showed her their credentials, Mrs. Evanston invited them in. The house was pleasant and bright. It was small but seemed in keeping with most of the others in this tiny mountain community. Mr.

Evanston worked in a larger town thirty miles to the south. Hank had made arrangements to interview him during his lunch hour.

Hank explained that they would like to question each child separately and would only be asking them to explain what they had seen. Mrs. Evanston would stay in the room during the questioning, but Hank asked that she not prod the children or answer for them. Hank made sure she knew that the children would not be pressured at all and if they seemed upset, Hank would not push for any information. Mrs. Evanston was fine with them talking to the children, so she called in her son, Billy, and introduced the agents. Billy seemed the epitome of a six year old boy. He sat in the chair but was fidgety.

"Billy, did you see something weird when you were in the woods with your family camping a few days ago?" Hank asked.

"You mean the monster? Yeah I saw that," Billy answered.

"Can you tell us what happened?" Hank asked.

Billy looked at his Mom as if for permission, shrugged his shoulders, and told his story. His family was on vacation. They were camping in the woods. They all went for a hike, and on the way back to camp, his dad told them to stop and be quiet. His dad pointed into the woods. Billy looked but couldn't see anything. He thought he heard something growl like Mrs. Brown's dog down the block sounds when he walks by with his friends on the way to the park. He didn't really see what made his Dad so upset. He could see some fur behind the bushes. "Maybe it was a bear. We have those here," Billy said. "I'm not supposed to go in the woods by myself 'cause bears can eat people if they get mad."

"Billy, do you like to draw pictures?" Hank asked

"Sometimes, if I have to stay inside 'cause it's raining."

"Well, I need to talk to your sister for a few minutes, but I sure would appreciate it if you could go in the other room and draw me a picture of what you saw," Hank requested.

"OK." Billy slid off his chair and headed down the hall.

Mrs. Evanston seemed relieved that the questioning of the children was so quick and easy. She called in her daughter and introduced the agents. Hank handled the situation much the same as he had with Billy. The daughter was a little older and had seen more. Her story was very similar to Billy's except for the fact that she saw the creature's face and described it as looking like a scary person's face, but with lots of hair everywhere. Again, Hank requested that she draw a picture of what she saw.

The questioning of Mrs. Evanston was much more extensive. Hank asked how long she had lived in the area, where she grew up, how long she'd known her husband, and those sorts of background questions. Then he asked her to explain why they were in the forest and the events leading up to her sighting of the creature.

She gave clear answers that sounded unrehearsed to Cassie. Mrs. Evanston had been afraid for the safety of her family when she saw the creature. She, like everyone in these parts, was well aware of the Bigfoot legend. Cassie asked some follow up questions being careful to stay within the guidelines learned during her BITES training. Before leaving the Evanston home, Hank collected the pictures the children had drawn.

They made a stop at the motel for coffee before heading to lunch with Mr. Evanston. A quick look at the children's drawings didn't prove anything but certainly depicted the scene they had described. On the way to lunch, Hank asked Cassie to give him her impression of the interviews.

"My assessment would be that they were all telling the truth. The children seemed to take it in stride which is reasonable for their ages and the fact that the creature didn't appear to pose any direct threat to the family."

"I agree. I believe they saw some kind of large beast. The daughter's comment about the face was probably the most substantial clue."

X X X

A few minutes before noon, they arrived at the small diner near the factory where Mr. Evanston worked as a line supervisor. They took a booth in the back corner and looked over the menu while they waited. Mr. Evanston walked in just after twelve o'clock and Hank made introductions. They placed their lunch orders before launching into the interview.

Mr. Evanston's story was much the same as his wife's. When he saw the creature, he didn't get a clear view but estimated it to be over seven feet tall with reddish brown hair. Like his daughter, he commented on the human-like quality of the face. Mr. Evanston said he looked right into the eyes of the creature and got the feeling it wasn't going to attack, though he couldn't explain why he felt that way. He and his family moved slowly away from the creature and headed back to their campsite.

"There was no way I could stay out there with the kids after that, so we packed up and came home."

Their food arrived and everyone ate with little conversation. Before Mr. Evanston finished eating, Hank asked some final questions. Had he ever seen a similar creature before? Did he believe that Bigfoot existed before he saw the creature? As with the rest of his family, Cassie got the sense that he was being honest and had been concerned for their safety.

After Mr. Evanston left, Cassie and Hank compared notes. She asked Hank why he didn't push for a more detailed description of the creature. He explained that he had learned from experience that doing so often led the interviewee to describe the creature they thought they had seen rather than describing only what they saw. "When we ask them to describe the events, we get the description the way they viewed it at the time, as though they were looking at the creature right then. It seems to work better than asking them to describe the creature they saw that they thought was Bigfoot because then they will describe Bigfoot instead of describing what they saw and letting us determine what it was."

Cassie learned a lot and enjoyed being part of a real investigation. It was much easier for her to imagine herself in the field, now that she had seen the BITES agents in action. The sky was overcast and threatening by the time they got back to the motel. "I hope you brought rain gear," Hank said as he parked the SUV.

"Should have thought of that, but I was so caught off guard when Mr. Meecham told me I was going on a field op, my mind wasn't really focused on my packing list," Cassie explained.

"I have to admit, it surprised me too. Don't get me wrong, I was happy, but surprised, or maybe impressed is a better word. Most people don't get sent into the field until the last couple of days of their fourth week of training and sometimes not even then. You just sailed through your training, so Mr. Meecham was anxious to see how you'd perform in the field."

CHAPTER THIRTY-TWO

Hank was at the small table in his room on his laptop typing up his report while Cassie sat on the bed checking email when Auggie, Grant, and Zuck returned. Everyone found a spot to sit and shared their impressions of the interviews they'd conducted. The general consensus was that the Evanston's had seen some large creature. Exactly what, might never be known, but Hank was going to recommend that the investigation continue to the next phase. He submitted his recommendation and the team starting making plans for heading into the forest the following day. Auggie made a list of the supplies they needed to pick up. They took the map down off the wall and determined where they would set up camp and the perimeter of the search area they planned to focus on.

Over dinner, Hank suggested they share stories of their best and worst investigation experiences to give Cassie an understanding of what being a BITES agent was really like. The laughter and camaraderie made Cassie feel like part of the team, but somehow she still got the impression that Zuck didn't think she'd be able to pull her own weight in the field. She was glad she'd have a chance to change his mind over the next few days.

After dinner, Hank suggested that he and Cassie shop for the supplies while the rest of the group returned to the motel. They drove to the small grocery store that was the only option in town. Cassie wondered if Hank offered to make the supply run so they could be alone for a few minutes.

"So Cass, do you have any concerns about heading into the forest tomorrow," Hank asked as they started down the produce aisle.

"I think I'm as prepared as I can be. Maybe the better question is whether or not you think I'm ready."

"If I didn't, I'd tell you, despite my personal feelings for you," Hank replied seriously.

"So you have feelings for me, huh," Cassie teased him.

"I guess my secret's out now. I thought I'd already made that pretty obvious. Apparently, I need to try harder. Seriously though, I won't ever do anything to put you or the team at risk."

"I know that," Cassie told him earnestly. "How much water do we need to get?"

The serious discussion over, they made sure they got everything on the list. After loading the groceries in the SUV, Hank took her in his arms and gave her a very long kiss.

"Oh, so those are the feelings you were talking about," she said as he released her.

"Those and much more," Hank said.

"I feel like I'm sneaking around behind my parents' back except it's the team not my folks."

Hank grinned, "I know what you mean."

X X X

The next morning they all ate a big breakfast before checking out of the motel and heading to the search area. It would be their last real food for a while. They climbed higher into the mountains with each passing mile. The thick moist air and ever-present gloom of the thick forests weighed Cassie down.

She was used to bright sunshine and long lines of sight in the desert. Somehow the whole mood of the place seemed dark and ominous. The air even smelled heavy. She and Hank drove the lead SUV with the three other agents in the second vehicle. Two hours after leaving the village, they had gone as far as they could drive. They parked the SUVs in a clear spot on the side of the road, picked up their packs, and made sure their guns were loaded.

"Here, Cassie," Zuck said handing her the largest dart gun. "You should carry Big Bertha. Since you're both girls, you two should get along real well."

Cassie accepted the heavy weapon, checked that it was loaded, and slung it over her shoulder. She knew this was some form of hazing from Zuck, but she had no qualms about handling "Big Bertha," so she said nothing. The group headed off down the trail to the location they had chosen for their campsite. After a few minutes, the easy banter amongst the group ceased as they fell into the rhythm of the hike.

The altitude was affecting Cassie a bit, but the cooler temperatures made it easier for her to push herself. Several times along the way, Cassie got the feeling that they were being watched. She'd stop and look around, but she never saw anything. She chalked it up to not being use to the environment and hoping that they'd actually see Bigfoot.

Just before noon, the path opened up into a small clearing. Remnants of a stone fire ring indicated others had used this area as a campsite.

Tents were erected and gear stowed. They ate a quick lunch of their most perishable supplies after which Hank got out the map and assigned search areas for the afternoon. Daylight lasted well into the evening this time of year, so they would go three hours out and have three hours to return to camp. Cassie and Hank would take the trail that led west out of the clearing. Auggie, Grant, and Zuck would follow the trail to the east. The teams checked in with each other via walkie-talkie every hour.

The trail narrowed, so Cassie followed behind Hank. The tree canopy was so thick Cassie doubted much sunlight would reach the ground if there was any sun in the gloomy skies overhead. The trail they were on stayed fairly level, gaining elevation gradually. Hank stopped often to look around and listen but they found no evidence and saw no creatures other than some insects that attracted Cassie's attention. She stooped to examine a slug and quietly asked Hank if he minded if she photographed it. She didn't see a lot of slugs in the desert of southern New Mexico. Later she found a snail and took a photo of it as well. It was another species not prevalent in the Desert Southwest. At one point, Hank signaled a stop thinking he'd seen movement off to the east, but neither he nor Cassie spotted anything. The other team wasn't having any better luck.

Both teams trudged into camp tired and disappointed at the end of the day. As they were eating dinner around the campfire, Hank held up his fist to stop the conversation. He'd heard a howl of some sort. Cassie had heard it too. They sat in silence for a few minutes but heard nothing further.

They talked quietly for a while longer and then called it a night, hoping for better luck tomorrow, when they could start their search at dawn. The teams normally set up two two-man tents, but adding Cassie to the mix meant they needed a third tent. She had a small one-person tent set up in between the other two. Auggie would be in with Hank and Grant shared a tent with Zuck. As Hank made his final check of the camp perimeter, he noticed an area at the edge of the forest that looked as though something large had been standing there for a long time. The grass was flattened and some small twigs were broken off the bushes and trees. He stopped by each tent and told them that he'd seen signs of an animal nearby, and they should keep their weapons handy. He made sure that Cassie was settled in before he went to bed himself after dousing the campfire and making a last check of the camp's perimeter.

CHAPTER THIRTY-THREE

Everyone was tired from the hike, so sleep came quickly and easily, except for Cassie. She needed to sleep well to be able to go even further tomorrow, but she had difficulty adjusting to the sounds of the forest. There are noises in the desert at night too but not as many or as varied. You might hear the howl of a coyote or the buzz of a cicada but that was about it. The forest sounded like the soundtrack from an old Tarzan movie.

She had just drifted off to sleep, or at least it seemed that way, when another of the loud howls they'd heard earlier woke her up. She checked her watch. It was a little after midnight. She pulled the pillow over her head and tried to go back to sleep.

She felt as though she had just closed her eyes again, when she heard a commotion in the campsite. There were sounds of rustling, tearing fabric, hollering, and running. She put on her boots, grabbed "Big Bertha" who'd been nestled in the tent beside her, and crawled out to see what was going on. Hank and Auggie were just coming out of their tent too. The other tent had been shredded. There was blood everywhere and no sign of Grant and Zuck.

Hank quietly told them to gear up with plenty of weapons and ammunition. "Remember night vision," he whispered.

Cassie ran back to her tent, threw on a sweatshirt, and grabbed the tranquilizer case, her rifle, and ammo.

Hank was scanning the tree line looking for some clue to tell him which way the men had gone when Grant came out of the forest waving his arms and yelling for them to help. He shouted, "Get the guns, we have to save him." They all looked at him. Hank squeezed Grants shoulder and stopped him in his tracks. "Grant, you have to slow down and tell us what happened," Hank said in a calm steady voice which even he was surprised to find he still possessed at that moment. Grant took a few deep breaths and Cassie handed him a bottle of water.

"We were in the tent sleeping. I woke up and the tent was ripped open and something was pulling Zuck out through the top. I threw my boots at it, but it ran into the woods. I tried to follow it, but without shoes or light I couldn't keep up and decided to come back for help. We have to hurry. It's running fast. Zuck was hollering at first but now he stopped. It's bad, Hank. It's really bad."

"We need to find Zuck," Hank shouted as he kept a hand on Grant's arm and led him back to the tents. Hank yanked out some clothes for Grant and his boots so he didn't have to go into the tent. He also handed him a pistol and an extra clip. "Make sure you bring the first aid kit and the camera as well as your weapons and plenty of ammo," Hank yelled as he grabbed things from his tent and tied his boots. "We head out in two minutes."

Hank and Auggie turned on their headlamps. Cassie and Grant carried flashlights. Once they had light, it was easy to spot the trail that the animal had taken. A few feet into the forest, Hank knelt down to touch something on the ground, he could smell the coppery scent of blood as he brought his fingers to his nose. He pointed it out to Auggie without saying anything. The trail of blood would lead them to Zuck. They ran as fast as the terrain and darkness would allow and a little faster.

Hank figured in his head that the animal had at least a five-minute head start, maybe more, but it was carrying a two hundred pound man. That should even the score a little, he hoped. They all ran on pure adrenalin. They weren't conscious of the passage of time or distance. Cassie no longer noticed any sounds except the breathing of her teammates.

They moved quickly but quietly not wanting to startle the animal. Hank signaled a stop to listen for any noise ahead of them on the trail. They heard nothing. Cassie got the feeling of being watched again. She stopped and looked around. She thought she saw movement in the woods to her left. She would swear she saw something move behind a large tree trunk, but she couldn't be sure. When she turned back to have Hank or Auggie take a look, she was alone. They had moved on down the trail not realizing that she had stopped.

Focus. We need to find Zuck. Bigfoot will have to wait, she told herself and moved off down the trail following the blood. She quickly caught up. The others hadn't realized she'd lagged behind.

Again, Hank signaled a stop, and they listened. They could hear a faint rustling in the woods ahead of them. It was impossible to tell how far away or know if it had anything to do with Zuck. They continued on more cautiously.

The fear was palpable. Cassie remembered she had the same feeling when she was abducted. It was like tunnel vision and tunnel hearing. She could hear nothing but her own heartbeat and was focused only on the men in front of her on the trail.

Analyzing it later, she came to the realization that it was a level of concentration you couldn't force yourself into unless in an extremely stressful situation. It was like a panic attack on steroids.

They moved around a large boulder and stopped short. Hank was facing a gigantic bear holding Zuck with one arm like he was nothing more than a bag of groceries. The bear looked at them as if sizing them up. It roared loudly.

The team stood like statues, desperately wanting to help Zuck and having absolutely no idea how to do so. Cassie knew that the longer they stood there, the more likely it was that someone would do something stupid, and it probably wouldn't be the bear. The howl they had heard before came again from the trees off to their left. They all turned to look in that direction. When they turned back, the bear and Zuck were gone.

Hank motioned for them to close ranks.

CHAPTER THIRTY-FOUR

"Let's take a breath everyone. It appears that we have two threats to worry about--the source of that howl and the bear. Auggie, you bring up the rear and have your rifle ready. Cassie I want you and Bertha up front. If you get a shot to bring down the bear without endangering Zuck, do it," Hank explained.

Grant moved with them but seemed to be completely shut down. He didn't speak. His eyes were huge. They herded him along between Auggie and Cassie.

Cassie had no idea whether they'd been running for five minutes or fifty. With all the adrenalin pumping through her body, she didn't notice being tired or thirsty or anything. They were all being scraped, scratched, and bitten by all manner of flora and fauna, but none of them noticed.

Hank signaled another stop. There were no sounds from the trail ahead. They moved forward still following the blood trail.

Hank stopped so quickly Cassie ran into his back and Grant into hers. They had climbed a small rise that looked down over a clearing. Cassie was sorry she looked. The biggest bear she had ever seen was in the clearing with one of its front paws pressed firmly in the center of Zuck's back. Zuck was face down on the ground and wasn't moving. Hank and Auggie backed away and moved behind Cassie. They were trying to make a plan without making any noise, communicating only with hand signals and gestures. Cassie collapsed onto her stomach and crawled to the edge of the hill. She had the large dart gun aimed directly at the bear's neck. She had intended to wait for Hank to give her the OK to shoot, but the bear took a swipe at Zuck's back opening up four large slashes. She knew she needed to act. She took aim, took a deep breath, exhaled, took another breath, and fired. The bear fell over backwards and lay still.

Hank and Auggie ran forward and saw that the bear was down. Hank ran down the hill and checked to make sure the bear was out. He signaled the others to come down. Auggie and Cassie checked Zuck's vitals. His pulse was strong but he was unconscious. He had several wounds from the bear's claws and teeth. Many of them would need stitches but none of them were bleeding too badly. Hank told Cassie to work on cleaning and dressing Zuck's wounds while he and Auggie figured out what to do with the bear. Grant just stood and stared.

Hank had hoped to move the bear away from Zuck, but they couldn't budge it. Instead they settled for gently moving Zuck away from the bear. Cassie and Auggie finished dressing Zuck's wounds, and Hank tried to wake him. They really needed him to walk out under his own steam or with limited assistance. They splashed some water in his face. He opened his eyes and looked around but didn't seem to be able to focus on anything before dropping back into the blackness. Hank talked to him and urged him to wake up. Zuck finally opened his eyes and seemed to recognize Hank. "Let's see if you can sit up," Hank said, helping Auggie to ease Zuck into a sitting position. He grimaced in pain but was able to sit up and drink some water. While they let Zuck recover a bit, Hank explained that they were going to get Zuck to his feet and with Hank on one side and Auggie on the other, they would head down the trail as quickly as possible.

"Cassie, as soon as we're moving, give the bear a double shot of tranquilizer with the injector, grab Grant and catch up with us," Hank explained. "Can you handle that?"

Cassie nodded and began prepping the two largest syringes. When she was ready she nodded to Hank. He and Auggie gingerly got Zuck to his feet and started up the hill. As soon as they started moving, Cassie administered the sedative, threw the used syringes into her pack and pulled Grant along. He followed, but he still wasn't talking.

They climbed up the hill and started running down the trail. Once they caught up with Hank, he talked with Grant briefly and that seemed to bring Grant back to a functional level. Hank asked Cassie to keep an eye on the trail behind them and have a dart gun ready. The trail narrowed to the point where three men side by side couldn't pass, so Hank and Auggie took turns assisting Zuck. It slowed down their progress but there was nothing else they could do.

When they approached the campsite, Hank explained the next step of the plan. "We need to get Zuck to the hospital as soon as possible. I know everyone is tried, but we have to move as fast as we can. We're not going to pack up the gear. We'll stop in camp just long enough for you to grab anything essential from the tents. Leave everything else. Once Zuck is stable, we can come back and get the gear."

Grant was doing better and even taking a turn assisting Zuck, but when they got back to camp, he shut down again. Seeing the destroyed tent seemed to bring it all back, and he wasn't handling it well. They were only in camp a couple of minutes before continuing on down the trail to where they had parked the SUVs. When the trail allowed, one man on each side of Zuck nearly carried him along. When the trail narrowed, their progress slowed.

When they reached the road, Hank handed Cassie the keys and asked her to run ahead, open the tailgate, and lay down the back seat so they could lay Zuck inside. All of them took any extra jackets, shirts, or clothing from their packs and their bodies and used them to make Zuck as comfortable as possible. Once they got him in the truck he shut his eyes and his breathing became very shallow. Cassie rode in the back to keep an eye on Zuck while Hank drove.

Auggie drove the other vehicle with Grant. It took hours, but they had no choice. Hank didn't believe any of Zuck's injuries were life threatening, but he wished he could get to the hospital quicker. The nearest hospital was in the town were Mr. Evanston worked, so they had to drive another thirty miles past their motel. When they reached the motel, Cassie called ahead to the hospital and let them know they were coming.

CHAPTER THIRTY-FIVE

The first fingers of light peeked over the mountains as Hank drove up to the emergency entrance of the local hospital. He ran in and explained the situation. In the meantime, Auggie and Grant parked and came over to help. They opened the tailgate to check on Zuck. Grant seemed much better. The drive must have given him time to calm down.

Hospital staff rushed out, loaded Zuck onto a gurney, and wheeled him into the ER. Hank suggested to Grant that he should get checked out too. He had lots of cuts on his feet from his barefoot run through the woods, but he refused. The team gathered in the waiting room. They took turns going to the bathroom to wash up. They were filthy and exhausted. Cassie and Hank made a run to the vending machines for coffee. It was bad coffee for sure, but at that stage it tasted like the nectar of the Gods.

With the adrenalin wearing off, Cassie found it hard to stay awake. Thankfully, the waiting room chairs were so uncomfortable it made it impossible to fall asleep. Cassie got up to walk around, and the nurse motioned her over to the desk.

"You all look like you've been attacked. I don't think there's one of you that isn't covered in blood. I know most of it is probably your friend's, but do you have any clean clothes with you?" she asked.

"I know we're a mess. We don't have any clean clothes. We used everything we had with us to make Zuck comfortable and bandage his wounds," Cassie explained

"I can try and scrounge up some scrubs so you can all take showers and clean up. It might be good to check that none of you have any cuts that need stitches while you're here. You all look like you've been in a footrace with the devil himself."

Cassie told Hank what the nurse had suggested, and they all took a look at each other. The nurse was right. They were probably frightening other patients. Cassie and Auggie went to the SUVs and dug through the packs to see if there were any clean clothes that weren't blood stained. They came up empty.

Cassie explained their situation to the nurse and said they'd be grateful for some clean scrubs and directions to the showers. In a few minutes, a nurses' aide brought them each a pillowcase with scrubs, shampoo, soap, first aid cream, and bandages. She showed them to the showers and told them the doctors were still working on their friend so not to rush.

A look in the mirror explained the staffs' interest in getting them cleaned up. The shower felt wonderful, but all the scratches and scrapes were painful when the water hit them. It felt good to be clean. Cassie had lots of scraps and cuts but nothing serious as far as she could tell.

The shower seemed to have revived them all. Grant had a few slashes that might have come from the bear when it attacked the tent, or they might just have been from running through the forest. Grant couldn't remember. The nurse cleaned them with antiseptic and bandaged them. She gave him some antibiotics to take in case they were from his battle with the bear.

When they were all together again back in the waiting room, Cassie took a look at them and smiled. "Now instead of looking like a family of serial killers, we look more like prison escapees, but I guess it's a step up."

They realized that if they had any clean clothes, they were at the campsite. They'd have to find somewhere local to buy the necessities to get them through at least a couple of days. Cassie talked to the nurse and found out where they would need to go.

About an hour later, a doctor came out and told them none of Zuck's injuries was life threatening, but he had lost a lot of blood. They had cleaned his wounds and sutured those that needed it.

Zuck was going to need a transfusion. They all volunteered to donate blood, but it was Cassie's blood that was a match. Zuck had been in and out of consciousness. He had some fractured ribs and a dislocated shoulder. They wanted to do the transfusion next and then run a few more tests before giving him a sedative to allow him to rest for the next several hours.

Between the adrenalin rush, the run through the forest, lack of sleep, and donating blood, Cassie was nearly out on her feet. The doctor said it would probably be later that evening before Zuck was awake and they could see him. There was a good chance he wouldn't wake up until morning. Hank said they should all head back to the motel and get some rest. The hospital staff had his cell number and would call if Zuck's condition changed. Hank needed to update Mr. Meecham and everyone needed some rest. They had gotten only a few hours sleep before the chaos began. "Do you want us to go get the gear?" Auggie asked.

"It can wait until tomorrow," Hank said. "Let's just get some sleep. We can figure out the plan when we aren't so tired."

Hank walked Cassie to her door. "Are you doing OK?" he asked.

"To be honest, I think I'm too tired to know. I knew working with Bites could be dangerous, but now I'm wondering if I'm really ready for this level of danger."

"I'm so sorry for all this. You were amazing. You realize that your shot probably saved Zuck's life."

"I just did what I was trained to do. Any of you could have taken that shot."

Hank didn't tell her that although she was right, any of them could have taken the shot, she was probably the only one who could have hit the target. They could talk about that tomorrow. "Don't take this the wrong way, but if you'd feel better not being alone, I can sleep in a chair in your room. Under the circumstances, no one will think anything of it."

"Thanks for the offer, but I'm fine," Cassie assured him. "Or maybe just too tired to know that I'm not, but either way, we all need to sleep. Do you have to send your report now or can you wait until you've had some rest," she asked, as concerned about him as he was about her.

"If any of Zuck's injuries were life-threatening, I would have called Meecham from the hospital so he could notify family, but at this point, I think it can wait a few hours. You sleep as long as you need. I'm going to set my alarm to be up at 2:00 PM so I can check on Zuck's status with the hospital and get a call in to Meecham. Just knock on my door whenever you're awake. We'll regroup and figure out a new plan." He leaned in and gave her a soft kiss before she closed her door.

She literally stepped out of her clothes on the way to the bathroom and nearly fell asleep before crawling between the sheets.

CHAPTER THIRTY-SIX

Cassie heard a ringing sound and reached over to turn off the alarm, but the ringing didn't stop. She tried again, but it still kept ringing. Then she remembered where she was. It wasn't her alarm ringing it was her cell phone. She answered and was surprised to hear Mr. Meecham's voice.

"Hello, Cassie. I just got off the phone with Hank and got his report on what happened with Agent Zuck. I wanted to check in with you and make sure you were doing OK," he said.

"Thanks for your concern, Mr. Meecham. I'm fine, just a little tired at the moment."

"My understanding is that you're something of a hero. Firing a shot to take down a large bear is quite a feat at any point, but to do so during your field training is exceptional. I'm sorry about what happened, but I am very proud of your performance," he rambled on.

"I know it sounds trite Mr. Meecham, but I just did as I was trained to do, as I'm sure any other BITES agent would have done. I thank you for your concern. If there's nothing else, I really need to grab a coffee and check in with the team. Good bye, Mr. Meecham," Cassie ended the call and sat on the edge of the bed, letting the events of last night run through her head. She felt terrible about what happened to Zuck. She was glad his injuries weren't severe, but she couldn't imagine how helpless he must have felt being carried off by a huge bear. Though she didn't know Zuck well, she felt sure helpless was not a feeling he was used to. It all seemed like a bad dream, but the pain in Cassie's feet assured her it had been all too real. Running miles in her hiking boots without socks had given her blisters on both feet. She took a quick shower, doctored her scratches and blisters, and got dressed. It struck her how easy it was to get dressed when you only had one change of clothes and no choices. She knocked on Hank's door, coffee in hand.

He answered the door and grabbed for the coffee like a man overboard grabbing for a life preserver. She walked into the room and noticed that the rest of the team wasn't there. "Thanks for the coffee. You're a real life saver," he said. He set the coffee down on the dresser and took Cassie in his arms. They stayed locked together for what seemed like several minutes, but Cassie knew was only seconds. He looked awful. He clearly needed more sleep and like Cassie, he had scratches, scrapes, and bruises covering all of his exposed skin which she couldn't help but notice since he was shirtless.

"Mr. Meecham called me. He said he had talked to you about what happened," Cassie explained. "How are you doing?"

"OK. As your training team leader I feel compelled to explain that most field work doesn't involve a situation like we experienced last night," Hank told her grasping the coffee cup like a lifeline. "It can happen, and that's why we train for it, but I want you to know this is the first time I've had anyone on my team injured by a biological during an investigation. I'm so sorry it happened during your first BITES field op."

Cassie was anxious to change the subject, "Have you heard from the hospital?"

"I checked on Zuck before I called Meecham. He's still sleeping. They say they expect he will awaken later tonight or tomorrow. He'll have some scars, but all the wounds are showing no signs of infection, which I guess is a big concern with bear attacks."

"What's our next move?"

"When the guys are awake, we'll make a plan, but I suggest we write up our official reports this afternoon while the events are still fresh in our minds. Anytime someone is injured on an op every BITES staff member who was involved or witnessed the event is required to file a formal report with Mr. Meecham. Other than that, we need to take the rest of the night to relax and get ourselves back on track. Tomorrow morning I'd like to go by the hospital to check on Zuck. If he's doing OK, we can drive out to retrieve our gear. Once we see how Zuck's doing, we'll be able to make decisions about when to head home. Some of you may be able to head back day after tomorrow, but some of us may need to stay if Zuck isn't able to travel that soon. We'll just have to play that by ear."

There was a knock on the door. Auggie came in and sat on the edge of the bed. He asked for an update on Zuck and what the plan was, just as Cassie had. When Hank finished getting Auggie up to speed, Grant joined them and they caught him up. Everyone returned to their rooms to write and submit their individual reports. Hank checked with the hospital again and was told Zuck was still asleep. Hank called the others and suggested they grab an early dinner and stop by the hospital to check on Zuck.

Everyone was still tired, and you could tell that each one was dealing with the events of the previous night in their own way. They tried to be lighthearted over dinner, but silence kept creeping back in as each person got lost in their own thoughts. The visit to the hospital did them all good. Zuck was sleeping but stirred when they entered his room as though he could sense their presence. He opened his eyes and looked at them. He looked puzzled when he got to Cassie, like he was trying to figure out how she fit in.

"Hi Zuck, buddy, do you know where you are?" Hank asked.

Zuck pointed to the water glass on his bedside table and Hank helped him get a drink. "It looks like I'm in a hospital," Zuck said.

"That's right. Do you remember what happened last night?" Grant asked.

"Not really. Am I OK? How did I get here?" Zuck asked. He sounded groggy and still out of it, but he seemed to recognize his teammates.

Hank didn't want to get into the details yet. He felt like Zuck would fall back asleep at any moment, so he simply said, "You were injured, and we brought you to the hospital. You're going to be fine, but you need to get some rest."

Zuck closed his eyes and was snoring softly within a minute. The team felt better having seen him wake up at least briefly.

"Let's meet for breakfast. We'll take both SUVs and check in on Zuck. Auggie and Grant, you can stay at the hospital with Zuck until we get back from retrieving the gear. We'll come back to the hospital to give you a break from bedside detail," Hank explained. "Zuck seemed like he might not have known who Cassie was, so I'm thinking he might have some short term memory loss. Probably just temporary, but I think it would be best if he woke up to faces he knew. Is everyone OK with that plan?"

"Sounds OK to me. Are you sure you two can manage all the gear?" Auggie asked.

"We'll be fine. We won't take anything with us but empty packs so we can load up everything. We'll get in and out as quickly as possible, just in case our furry friend has a better memory than Zuck," Hank assured them. Auggie and Grant headed for their rooms to crash, leaving only Cassie and Hank.

"Are you doing OK with all this?" Hank asked. "This has got to be stressful for you. Anything you want to talk about?"

"Honestly, I'm fine. I've been involved with search and rescue work at the BLM. Though I've never had someone on my own team attacked, I have seen lots of injuries and some pretty dreadful things. I think you learn to compartmentalize so you can keep going," Cassie explained. "I'm just glad Zuck is going to be OK and the rest of us are fine."

"Has anyone ever told you how amazing you are, Cassie Carter?" Hank asked pulling her into an embrace.

"Not nearly enough," she answered as they shared a heated kiss. "I think I'd better head back to my room if I want to get any sleep tonight," Cassie said as she backed away. "I'll see you in the morning."

CHAPTER THIRTY-SEVEN

Hank's head was reeling. He knew it wasn't wise to get into a romantic relationship with Cassie when she was working with his team and especially after what the team had been through the past few days, but sometimes logic and feelings didn't play in the same arena. She was the most interesting woman he'd ever met. He thought she might be someone he could spend his life with. That realization scared him more than any bear attack ever could. He needed to focus on the team, but at the moment that included Cassie which sent his thoughts careening in a hundred different directions again.

At breakfast, everyone was getting back to normal. There was more conversation and laughter. Zuck was awake and sitting up when they got to the hospital.

"How are you feeling?" Hank asked when they all trooped into Zuck's room.

"I'm doing OK, but my arms and shoulder hurt like hell," Zuck complained. "Are one of you going to tell me what happened?"

Grant started the story, since he had been in the tent with Zuck when the bear attacked. Hank picked up the story at the point where the rest of the team heard the noise and ran after him.

"So I really got carried away by a bear," Zuck said. "The nurse told me that, but I can't remember it at all. I thought she was just joking around because something worse had happened."

"I'm not sure what you'd classify as worse than being carried off by a bear, but that's what happened," Grant said. "And Cassie saved your ass, so you'd better be nice to her."

Zuck looked at Cassie. "I'm sorry, I really don't remember you, but if these guys are telling the truth, I guess I owe you."

"We just met a couple of days ago," Cassie explained. I'm in training with BITES and was assigned to your team for my field training."

"So how did you save me?" he asked.

"I didn't really save you. I followed orders and shot the bear with a tranquilizer dart," she explained.

"What she's not telling you," Auggie said, "is that she dropped the bear with one shot. Hit it perfectly in the neck. Then she covered our backs while we took turns lugging your sorry ass back to the SUVs in the dark. Then just to be sure she stole all the glory, she donated the blood they used for your transfusion."

"Well, thanks Cassie. I look forward to getting to know you, again," Zuck said. "I'm really tired guys. Can you let me get some sleep?"

"Sure thing," Hank replied. "Some of us will be in the waiting room if you need anything. Just have the nurse come get us."

X X X

Zuck was asleep before they reached the hallway. Auggie and Grant headed to the hospital cafeteria for coffee before settling into chairs in the waiting room. Cassie and Hank headed back to the forest to retrieve the gear they left during their run to safety the previous morning.

After seeing that Zuck was recovering, the team felt as though a weight had been lifted. Cassie and Hank talked all the way to the forest, and it was pleasant as it had always been when they weren't running for their lives. They talked about their relationship, though neither of them was really comfortable doing so. They both realized that going through a traumatic event together made them feel closer to each other than the time they'd been involved would warrant. Each of them was looking for a long-term committed relationship, but they seemed to have difficulty putting anything more into words.

They parked the SUV off the road, and Cassie put on an extra heavy pair of socks to cushion her sore feet before heading in to the campsite. "We're going to get in and out of there as quickly as possible," Hank explained as they started the hike. "I don't expect to see the bear, but I don't want to take any chances."

"Do we need to do anything special with Grant and Zuck's tent since it's evidence of the attack?" Cassie asked.

"We'll take it with us, but we don't need to treat it any differently than the others," Hank said.

X X X

When they got to the campsite, they both pulled up short. Seeing the damage to the tent in the daylight, it looked much worse than they remembered. They shook it off and started loading up the packs. By mutual, unspoken agreement, they left the damaged tent for last. As they packed it up, they noticed the blood on Zuck's sleeping bag and on the tent where the bear had pulled him through. It made them both realize how lucky Zuck and all of them had been.

They stood surveying the empty campsite before starting the hike back. Hank had his arm around Cassie's shoulders. "Is this going to affect your decision to work for BITES?" he asked.

"Of course not," Cassie stated. "I'll admit I was shaken up yesterday when I stopped to think about everything that happened out here, but I knew the work could be dangerous when I accepted the position. Any job that puts you out in the wilderness comes with the risk of an animal attack."

Hank looked thoughtful. "I'm not sure what I was hoping you'd say. On the one hand, I'm glad that you're determined to continue with BITES. It's something we share, and that's a good thing. On the other hand, pursuing a relationship might be easier if we didn't both work for BITES. Oh hell, I don't know what I'm saying or thinking at this point. Let's get out of here and head back to town. Maybe I'll find my sanity somewhere along the way."

On the drive to the hospital, Cassie realized that in the past few months this was the second time she found herself in a very dangerous situation. It gave her a perspective she didn't have before. She knew her abduction had changed her, and now the attack on Zuck was reminding her that she should never let an opportunity for happiness pass her by.

When they stopped at the hospital, they were happy to see Zuck sitting in a chair talking with Auggie. He still couldn't remember the attack or his escape, but otherwise he was getting back to normal. The doctor said that he would check all of Zuck's stitches in the morning and if all was well, he'd be released and the team could fly home.

"Do you think the bear that attacked Zuck is what the Evanston's saw?" Cassie asked on the way back to their motel.

"I doubt we'll ever know," Hank answered. "It wasn't as tall as they described, and I would expect most folks who live around here to recognize a bear if they saw one, but we'll never know for sure."

CHAPTER THIRTY-EIGHT

Cassie and Hank both realized that the emotionally charged situation they'd shared had brought them closer. They avoided talking about Cassie's fast approaching return to New Mexico. When Hank dropped her off at the lodge, he asked when her flight home was. She told him it was scheduled for early Monday morning. "If you'd like, you're welcome to spend the weekend at my condo. I have a spare bedroom, if you want it," Hank explained.

"I'm not quite sure how you mean that, but I'm thinking we have a lot to talk about and should take advantage of every minute. When we finish up at the lodge on Friday, let's head to your place," Cassie agreed. She would not normally have been so impulsive, but she and Hank needed to talk about their relationship before she returned to New Mexico. She knew that Hank would allow her to sleep in the guest room if that was her choice.

X X X

"Cassie, I'm glad I got to talk to you. I wanted to find out how you were feeling about your decision to join BITES now that your training is complete. I can't tell you how sorry I am that you had such an unfortunate event occur during your field training," Mr. Meecham explained. Cassie had received a note during breakfast and found herself in his office once again.

"I enjoyed the training and feel I'm well prepared for field work. While the incident in Washington was unfortunate, I feel the team handled it well," Cassie said. "I'm proud to be part of BITES and anxious to start working with my team in the southwest."

"I'm glad to hear that. Everyone here has grown very fond of you and has been impressed with your skills on every front. I must tell you that your shot that took down that bear is becoming legendary throughout BITES. I've even heard that Mr. Zuck is singing your praises and that may be your most impressive feat yet," Mr. Meecham said with a rare smile. "You may consider your training complete and yourself on active duty. I am looking forward to a long association with you and will be anxious to hear about your next field operation. Good luck, Cassie. I look forward to reading your reports."

Cassie found Hank in the team office and told him she was finished and they could head home whenever he was ready. She went to her room, packed up her belongings, and waited for him in the sitting area until he finished for the day. They loaded her luggage into his truck and headed for his home near the city.

X X X

Hank showed her around his place. Large dark furniture seemed to be his chosen style. Nothing was cluttered. It was very nice, but you could tell it was home to a bachelor. Décor was limited to photos of cryptids tacked up on the wall above his desk with pushpins. He explained that he didn't want too much to take care of since his work with BITES sometimes kept him away for weeks at a time. The condo was the best option for his current situation. There were two bedrooms and two baths which was convenient when his family came to visit. They put Cassie's luggage in the guest room and headed out to dinner.

Over a delicious meal at a small family-run Vietnamese restaurant, they made plans for the next two days. Afterward they stopped at the grocery for supplies. Back at Hank's they put away their purchases, and Hank told Cassie he needed a few minutes to catch up on some things. Cassie checked email and found a message from her Mom asking how the training was going and wanting to hear more about this "Hank" she seemed to be spending so much time with. *No matter how old you are, moms still act like moms*, Cassie thought with a smile. Bob emailed to say that her apartment was waiting for her return and they'd get together someday next week for lunch so she could tell him all about her training.

Hank walked into the living room, "Cass, I got an email from Zuck. He seems to be doing better although he still can't remember anything from going to bed that night in the tent until he woke up in the hospital the next day. He's still trying to come to terms with the idea that a 'girl' saved him."

Cassie just shook her head with a smile. They snuggled up on the sofa and watched a bad sci-fi movie. They made fun of the dialogue and laughed a lot. It had been a pleasant, comfortable evening. When the movie ended, Hank turned off the TV, gave Cassie a passionate kiss, and said he was going to bed, "I'd love to have you join me, but I'll understand if you choose not to. No pressure."

Cassie sat on the sofa a few minutes after Hank left weighing her options and trying to decide whether to be logical or impulsive. Should she follow her heart or her head? In the end, she fell asleep on the sofa without making a decision.

X X X

Hank walked into the kitchen early in the morning to make coffee and found Cassie curled up on the sofa. He smiled at the scene, got a blanket off the guest bed, noticing that it hadn't been slept in, he covered her up, and headed for the shower.

Cassie awoke to the smell of coffee brewing. It took her a moment to realize where she was. She laughed out loud at the circumstance. She felt slightly embarrassed by the situation, but Hank was smiling at her as he handed her a cup of her favorite coffee. She smiled back. "I'm so sorry," was all she could think of to say. Hank got his own coffee and sat down next to her on the sofa.

"Are you OK?" he asked.

"OK, but a little embarrassed," Cassie admitted with a grin.

"What happened? Did something wake you or was the bed in the guest room not comfortable?" Hank inquired, grinning to himself. He had a pretty good idea what had happened, but he didn't plan on letting her off the hook that easily.

"OK, I'm not awake enough to come up with any plausible story," Cassie said, "so I'll admit the truth. After you went to bed last night, I sat here trying to decide if I should join you or not. My logical side was telling me we're great friends and I shouldn't mess that up, but your kiss and my emotions were saying that we both wanted something more. Then I started wondering if it would make it easier or harder to leave on Monday. Then there's the complication of working together. Ugh! All of this stuff was running around my head, and I guess I just fell asleep. I'm really sorry, but we knew we needed to talk about this stuff anyway."

"I won't lie. I was disappointed that you didn't join me last night. I'm sorry you're feeling so conflicted," Hank assured her. "But you're right, we need to talk about where this is going before you leave. Maybe we should just get that out of the way now, so we can enjoy the rest of our weekend."

They both admitted they had feelings for each other and would like to see how things might develop. Hank convinced

Cassie that BITES wasn't an issue. Except for the rare circumstance like last week's training, or if he were on a case involving insects, they would not likely be working together on an investigation. BITES did not have any policy about fraternization, and he felt they were both adult enough to act professionally if one of those situations arose. The big elephant in the room was the distance. Both of them would have crazy schedules as BITES agents. They agreed that maintaining any relationship would be difficult but convinced themselves and each other that at least if you were dating another BITES agent, then you both should understand the scheduling issues. They were both able to afford to travel for weekend visits when their schedules permitted.

Hank sat his coffee cup down on the table and turned to face Cassie. "So it seems to me that we have eliminated all the obstacles. Do you want to give it a go and see where this relationship leads?" he asked.

Cassie answered with a kiss. He responded by taking her hand and leading her into the bedroom. So much for their plans for the day. Later that morning they headed out to spend time in the mountains. Cassie felt great. She was happy and relaxed, and Hank appeared to be quite pleased with how things had worked out. Since they were getting a late start, he suggested they not drive too far, but hike a trail that was only a few miles from the city. They talked, held hands, and acted like giddy teenagers, but it was fun. Sometimes, Cassie thought, being an adult sucked all the fun out of everything.

Back in town, they stopped and picked up a coffee maker for Hank's, so she could have her favorite coffee when she was in town. Anyway, he'd become hooked on the stuff himself, he admitted. Cassie realized it was a gesture meant to assure her she'd be coming back and spending more time at the condo. It worked. She felt good about where this was going though she was trying not to run through all the what-ifs in her head over and over. One thing she knew for sure was that she didn't intend to fall asleep alone on Hank's sofa again.

CHAPTER THIRTY-NINE

Hank left Cassie at the airport on Monday morning with a smile on her face and the promise that they'd talk everyday unless one of them was in the field. She spent the flight home thinking about all that had happened in the past few months. Life was good at the moment. She knew there would be bumps along the way, but she was glad to find herself in a good place for now.

X X X

"Hi, Bob, it's great to see you," Cassie said, standing to give Bob a hug when they met for lunch later in the week. "Tell me what I've missed."
"Same old same old here. A couple of lost hikers found safe. Jeremy driving me crazy, Cory complaining about how much paper we use. Pretty much the same as when you left," he told her. "But that smile on your face tells me you have a lot to fill me in on."

Cassie talked for the next forty minutes, barely taking time to eat her lunch. Bob asked many questions, but mostly grinned like a proud parent listening to the accomplishments of one of his children. As they prepared to leave, they decided they'd make this a standing date every week.

X X X

When Cassie returned home, she emailed Jim Lansing and her teammates telling them she had completed her training and was ready when an assignment came their way. Jim emailed back that he'd received a report on her training from Meecham and was impressed with all of her training scores. He'd also been informed about the situation during her field training and said to call him if she wanted to talk about the incident further.

Cassie got into the habit of doing her fitness routine every morning before breakfast then settling in to do research. She started by researching all the cryptids that had ever been reported in New Mexico. She wasn't sure there'd be any and was shocked that there were several. She hadn't been aware that the Jemez Mountains west of Santa Fe were a hotbed for Bigfoot sightings. *Maybe Hank's team will be sent to investigate sometime*, she mused. There was the Mogollon Man on the eastern edge of the state extending into Arizona. It sounded like this creature was similar to Bigfoot in many ways. Of course, Chupacabra reports throughout the southwest, including New Mexico, were fairly common. She was sure that she'd heard stories about Bigfoot and Chupacabra but she didn't know anything about them because she had assumed the stories were fake. Now she was feeling the need to re-evaluate.

She'd been home less than two weeks and had developed a good routine. She did her fitness run most days before breakfast, ran any errands, and did emails, then spent the rest of the day doing research on line until time for dinner. After dinner, Hank called, and they talked for hours. It surprised her how much she missed him and how anxious she was to figure out when they could see each other again.

She checked in with her teammates daily via email, and they shared what they were researching at the time. Jim emailed anytime there were sightings in the southwest that they needed to keep tabs on.

Bob called one afternoon to ask if she wanted to join in the search for a party of three hikers that had gone missing in the desert east of Las Cruces. She called Jim to make sure it was OK for her to participate. He explained that it was a great idea to stay involved with the local search and rescue squads. It was a good way for BITES agents to get involved in their community and put their outdoor skills to good use.

CHAPTER FORTY

Cassie packed up her gear, dressed in her BITES shirt, took her Homeland Security credentials, and headed to the search command area. She knew all of the searchers, and they were happy to have her assistance. No one even asked to see her identification, which was a little disappointing, if truth be told. Everyone was used to Cassie working with Bob, so she was grouped with him and Jeremy and assigned an area to search. Three hikers, all young men, headed out to explore the old ghost town and the surrounding mining areas. They had some experience in the desert, and as far as anyone knew, should have had plenty of supplies with them. They were supposed to return home in the evening two days ago. Yesterday morning when their friends realized that none of them had been heard from, they were reported missing.

It was great to be working with Bob again, and Jeremy was OK, but Cassie admitted that BITES methods were very different. They were much more methodical. She utilized her new skills where she could, and Bob let her take the lead. They received word that some gear believed to belong to the missing hikers had been found just to the north of their search area. Cassie suggested that they take a route on the north side of their assigned quadrant to take them closer to where the gear had been found.

Late that afternoon, Cassie's group rounded some rocks and dropped down into a secluded arroyo. They pushed through the thick mesquite and creosote bushes into a large clearing. They all froze. The scene in front of them looked like something out of a slasher movie. Cassie didn't think she'd ever forget the smell. The vegetation was trampled. Body parts and bones lay scattered around the area. There were damp spots on the ground that Cassie knew were probably blood. She and Bob made mental notes of the number of limbs they could identify while Jeremy retreated back through the curtain of vegetation and deposited his lunch onto a prickly pear cactus.

Cassie and Bob figured there were parts of at least two different bodies in the clearing. Bob radioed their position and situation to the command post, while Cassie started flagging the evidence. Bob joined her, and they expanded the search outward marking everything they found that might be of interest. Bob hollered to Jeremy to stay outside the clearing so he didn't contaminate the scene. Jeremy directed the other searchers to their location. By the time the other search teams arrived, the scene had been secured and the searchers waited for the CSIs and the coroner to give them some indication of whether the three missing men were here, or if they needed to continue the search. The coroner and his assistant arrived and quickly determined that the clearing contained the partial remains of at least three men. Preliminary examinations of the remains showed them to be a match for the missing hikers at least by age and ethnicity, anything more definitive would have to wait until they got the remains back to the lab. Several of the more experienced searchers, including Bob and Cassie, were enlisted to photograph all of the evidence and help bag and tag everything. Cassie was assigned to take the photos. As she finished with an area, Bob and the others would gather and tag the evidence in that area while Cassie photographed the next gruesome scene.

It was a long, hot, depressing afternoon. By the time Cassie arrived home, she just wanted a shower and to talk to Hank. She filled him in on the search and discovery. He reminded her that she should make a full report of her involvement to Jim. If they found out that the Thunderbird had been the cause of this attack, it was likely the BITES team would be activated soon. Hank explained that sometimes the red tape involved with getting BITES participation in an investigation could take some time, so not to expect anything to happen too soon. He told her he missed her and was anxious to figure out when they would see each other again. They said good night, and Cassie crashed on the sofa.

She woke up at midnight, ate an English muffin pizza, and went to bed. After her run the next morning, she checked the local news and her email, but there were no updates on the missing hikers. It would be at least another day before the coroner released his findings.

She brewed her first cup of coffee and sat down at the computer to write her report. After she emailed Jim, she headed out to run some errands. She felt antsy. She hated the thought that her discovery might be responsible for the deaths of more people, but deep down she knew that was the mostly likely explanation. On the other hand, she was excited that she might be involved in a BITES field op on her home turf.

One of her stops was to pick up the weapons BITES had shipped to her. It was difficult to transport weapons on airplanes these days, and since there had been no immediate need for her to have access to them, Mr. Meecham shipped her assigned weapons. Jim had provided instructions on turning an ordinary closet into a secured weapons' locker and she made all the necessary preparations while waiting for the shipment to arrive.

As Cassie unpacked the firearms into her locker at home, she got that surreal feeling again. As a competitive shooter,

Cassie always had guns in her home and was very methodical about keeping them locked up securely, but once all the items were in place, it looked like something you'd see in the movies. It was that scene where the ex-special forces guy pushed to his limits by the injustices of the world, goes into his cellar and reveals a hidden room with enough firepower to stage a coup on a small island nation.

Cassie had completed all the necessary paperwork and had all her permits in order, but it seemed excessive for a home arsenal, even to her. She closed the door and checked the cipher lock that had been installed. Her condo association had not been happy about the modifications to the closet, but a letter from Homeland Security persuaded them to allow it.

When the coroner's report definitively identified the three missing men from the body parts that had been found, the official cause of death was listed as an animal attack. Details of the report indicated the animal responsible was a large bird such as the Thunderbirds. Damn. Cassie knew this was likely, but had held out hope that some other cause would be found.

She emailed Jim the results and copied Hank so he'd know what was going on. Bob called, after he read the report, to see how she was doing. He knew she'd feel responsible.

She knew it was irrational, but she couldn't help the way she felt. Deep down, she knew even if she hadn't found the birds, someone would have, and the outcome might have ended up the same, but that didn't make it any easier to stomach. She was tough, but she wasn't heartless. The recent tragedies around her were starting to take a toll, though she would never admit that to anyone.

CHAPTER FORTY-ONE

Several days later when Hank called, he told her he had some good news. He was coming to New Mexico to investigate a new Bigfoot sighting near Santa Fe. With Zuck still out on medical leave, Mr. Meecham had suggested that Cassie join the team for the investigation since she'd worked with them before. Hank would be flying into Albuquerque in the morning. The rest of the team wouldn't arrive until the following day. Cassie and Hank would have a day and night to catch up before the op got started in earnest. While she talked with Hank, an email arrived from Mr. Meecham explaining the situation and asking her to join Hank's team for the op. Hank texted his flight info and said he couldn't wait to see her.

Cassie shifted into high gear. She starting laying things on the bed that she needed to pack. She emailed Bob explaining she'd be out of town and asking him to check on her condo. She sent Hank a text to find out if she should bring any of her weapons along. She replied to Mr. Meecham that she would meet Hank's team in northern New Mexico. She checked the email from Meecham and saw that he'd copied Jim Lansing, so she didn't need to notify him. She called her Mom and filled her in on the plans.

"At some point, you're going to need to tell me more about Hank. What does he look like?" her mom asked.

"I guess I'd describe Hank as ruggedly handsome. He's very intense," Cassie said with a laugh. She tried to picture Hank in her head, but kept coming up with mental pictures she definitely shouldn't be sharing with her mother.

"That's great, but what does he look like?"

Well, he's over six feet tall. He has black hair and brown eyes."

"How's he built?"

"Mom! I don't think that's appropriate. I will say he's very muscular, and that's all I'm saying."

"I'm old, Cassie. I'm not dead. He seems to have become a large part of your life lately," her Mom chided.

"We'll have a long talk about that soon, I promise, but I need to get packed and get some sleep. I have to be on the road early. I'll call when I can."

Hank texted that she should bring all of her weapons. They could purchase ammo in Albuquerque. Cassie opened the "arsenal" as she called it, and packed up her gear. She didn't sleep well. She was excited to see Hank and to be on another assignment, but she was a little wary about how any of the team would react to being back in the woods after their last experience. She believed whole-heartedly in facing your fears, so she felt getting back on the horse was the best option. She was excited to go on another field op, but in the back of her head, she wondered if she was becoming an adrenalin junkie.

X X X

Cassie was on the road enjoying her coffee and the beautiful New Mexico sunrise by 5:30 AM. Unable to sleep, she figured she might as well get an early start.

It was her turn to be waiting for Hank in baggage claim. His flight was only a few minutes late. She couldn't believe how great it was to see him again. It had only been a few weeks, and they talked daily, but it seemed like a long time since they were together. After an appropriate welcome, they retrieved his luggage, loaded it into Cassie's SUV, and headed out of the Albuquerque Sunport.

"Where to now?" Cassie asked. "I'm not sure what the plan is for today."

"Let's stop, grab a good breakfast, and I'll fill you in."

Cassie stopped at a local Albuquerque breakfast spot. They both placed their orders for breakfast burritos and coffee. "Red or green," the waitress asked Cassie.

"None, neither. Thanks," Cassie said.

When the waitress turned to Hank with the same question, he gave Cassie a questioning look. "Red, green, or Christmas?" the waitress prompted.

"She wants to know if you want red or green chili or both," Cassie explained. "It's a New Mexico thing."

Hank ordered green chili on his breakfast burrito.

"The team isn't arriving until tomorrow. I thought we'd pick up the ammo we need here. I have directions to a gun shop. Then we can head up to Santa Fe, check into our hotel, and enjoy the evening. When the guys arrive, they'll rent an SUV and meet us at the hotel."

"Are there any interviews scheduled for today?" Cassie asked.

"Nope, today is just for us to spend some time together. Work starts tomorrow," Hank replied, reaching across the table to take her hand. "I've missed you, Cass."

On the drive to Santa Fe, they discussed their past relationship history. When you were in a new relationship, Cassie felt you were obligated to have this discussion, but she wasn't sure why. She didn't really want to know about Hank's past loves and couldn't believe he wanted to know about hers either, but it was a socially accepted practice, so they dove in.

Neither one had much to tell. Hank, being a few years older, had been in a couple of serious relationships, but both ended when he realized the women weren't the right choice for him long term. Cassie explained her breakup with Tony the same way. She realized he wasn't the person she wanted to spend her life with. Neither of them understood why so many relationships seemed to have such a high drama quotient. Cassie agreed with Hank's assessment that, "if it's right, it should be easy."

They checked into their hotel and went for a walk around the Santa Fe Plaza. They returned to their room and spent the afternoon getting reacquainted. Much later that day, Cassie extricated herself from Hank's arms and grabbed a quick shower. She smelled the coffee brewing when she came out of the bathroom. Hank was up, dressed, and smiling as he handed her a mug. They headed out to catch the fabulous Santa Fe sunset from the second floor patio of a restaurant on the plaza. The sunset was gorgeous, the food delicious, and the company perfect. Cassie realized she was more content with Hank than she had ever been with anyone else. That realization scared her a little.

X X X

The next day, Cassie checked into her room before Grant and Auggie arrived. She and Hank decided they wanted to maintain their professional relationship in front of the team. They didn't want to make anyone uncomfortable, including each other. They agreed that when the investigation concluded Hank would try to stay in New Mexico another day or two so they could have more time together.

Hank and Cassie scheduled the interviews before the guys arrived. Auggie and Grant greeted Cassie warmly and said they were happy to be working with her again. After grabbing lunch and handing out the assignments, Cassie and Hank headed out to interview the person who had reported the sighting. This time it was a hiker who had been alone at the time. The retired man lived in Santa Fe. His report sounded fake to Cassie, but she couldn't explain why. During the questioning, his story changed many times, and when they finished, both she and Hank agreed this was not a valid sighting.

Their next interview was with a ranger at Valles Caldera National Preserve northwest of Santa Fe. On paper, he was a credible witness. He reported a sighting a few weeks ago in almost the same area as the retired hiker. Hank explained that because there were so many Bigfoot sightings all over the US, BITES couldn't investigate them all. Unless a sighting was reported by multiple witnesses at the same time or there was photographic or other hard evidence, reports often languished until another sighting in the same area made it worth sending the team to investigate.

Though she preferred the desert, Cassie agreed that Valles Caldera was a beautiful spot. The 13 mile wide volcanic crater is one of only six super volcanoes in the world. There is still a great deal of geothermal activity in the area with many hot springs. The caldera valley supports the largest elk herd in New Mexico. Ranger Rick, really that was his name, gave a very detailed account of his encounter even though it happened several weeks earlier. It was clear that he had told the story several times and that he wasn't making it up. Much like the Evanston's in Washington, Ranger Rick believed he saw Bigfoot, and no one could change his mind.

CHAPTER FORTY-TWO

Hank's team met over dinner and compared notes from their interviews. The consensus was that the retired gentleman was either confused or made a fraudulent report to gain attention. Ranger Rick's sighting, however, appeared to be factual. That's not to say that he saw Bigfoot, but he certainly saw something that to him, looked like Bigfoot. The team decided since there had been many credible sightings of Bigfoot in the caldera area over the years, they'd spend a few days in the forest to see if they could find any hard evidence of the creature's existence.

Auggie and Grant excused themselves before dessert, claiming they needed to return to their rooms to make phone calls home. Cassie knew Grant was married and Auggie had a girlfriend, but she got the feeling they left so that she and Hank could be alone. When she said as much over dessert, Hank admitted he'd told Auggie about their relationship. Auggie was his best friend, so it just wasn't possible to keep it from him. Hank hadn't said anything to Grant, but suspected Auggie might have clued him in. Even though the team knew, Cassie thought they still should maintain some propriety on the job, and Hank agreed. He walked her back to her room and kissed her good night.

X X X

After breakfast, they checked-out, loaded up their gear, and headed for the Caldera. When they stopped at the visitor's center, Hank showed Ranger Rick the map with all the Bigfoot sightings marked. The majority of them were definitely grouped in one section of the Preserve, so Hank asked Ranger Rick to suggest the best place to camp close to that area and the best trails to explore. The team followed the access road as far as possible, parked the SUVs and loaded up their packs. Cassie hated to admit it but she was feeling a bit of déjà-vu, and it was giving her goose bumps despite the warm temperature.

When they reached the GPS coordinates Ranger Rick had provided, they found some level ground and setup camp. They had only taken two tents. Hank and Cassie would share one tent. Grant and Auggie the other.

With several hours of daylight left, they decided to recon some of the trails in the area. Hank and Cassie headed west. while Auggie and Grant went east. They would meet back at camp in time to make dinner before dark. After what happened to Zuck, they wanted to take all possible precautions to avoid a similar situation. This time they brought no perishable food that might attract wildlife--only MREs, protein bars, and that sort of thing.

Hank and Cassie looked for any evidence that a large animal had been on the trail, footprints, branches snapped off, fur snagged on a bush. The only discernable tracks they found were elk which wasn't surprising. It was nice to be outdoors with Hank again, just the two of them. Cassie felt weird that she was spending more time in the field with Hank's team when she had yet to spend any time in the field with her own team, but she knew that would change.

Auggie and Grant came up empty as well. Auggie found some broken off branches, but the location of them made it inconclusive. They found nothing else of interest. Around the campfire, Cassie asked them to tell her about the eradication part of a field op. So far, she'd been involved in the investigation part, but had no experience with eradication.

The three experienced agents agreed that was how it normally worked. Lots of investigating and very little eradicating. Hank explained, "Over my career with BITES I've learned the ratio is about ten to one. The problem is the creatures we hunt are elusive. That's why you don't see a Bigfoot in every zoo. So for every ten to fifteen cases we investigate, we may actually see one cryptid. Even though we see it, that doesn't mean we will get to the stage of eradication.

"The way it's supposed to work is we track an animal then use the dart guns and nets to secure it. Then we call the office and arrange transport. The only time I was involved with an eradication in the past two years, they sent a chopper that lowered a crate to us. We got the sedated animal into the crate, and the chopper took it away. I've never asked what happened next. I know they'd like us to capture the creatures rather than kill them because they want to study them, but I'm not sure what they hope to learn. I do it because I want people to know the truth and be safe in the wilderness."

When Hank finished, they all applauded. He laughed, "I know, down off the soapbox before I get hurt."

When they had packed away all the food, Cassie spoke what had been on everyone's mind, "Do you think any of us will be able to sleep tonight?"

"We can only try," Auggie said with a sigh. And with that, they all crawled into their tents and tried to close their eyes. Cassie got into her sleeping bag and snuggled up to Hank with her head on his shoulder and his arm around her. She felt safe and comfortable, but it was still hard to get the vision of the torn and bloody tent from their last field op out of her mind. She heard Auggie and Grant's muffled voices talking for a long time. Hank kissed her good night, and she eventually fell asleep.

When she awoke he was stroking her hair and watching her sleep. Cassie knew by the light that it was morning, and the night had passed without incident, thank God.

CHAPTER FORTY-THREE

Today the team would split up with each pair following a trail parallel to the other. If either group spotted anything of interest, the other agents could cut through the woods and meet up with them in short order. The morning passed with no findings. Because it stayed daylight so late this time of year, they could hike a couple of hours after lunch before needing to start back to camp.

Cassie motioned for Hank to stop and pointed to a trail branching off to the right toward the trail that Auggie and Grant were on. It wasn't on their map and was probably a game trail. Some hair stuck to a broken branch about seven feet off the ground, caught Cassie eye. They explored the vegetation at the corners where the paths merged. Broken branches were visible at about the same height on each side of the cross trail. Cassie photographed the trail intersection, the broken branches, and the hair stuck in the branch. Hank pulled a baggie from his cargo pants pocket and retrieved the hair. It was coarse and orangish in color, but there was no way to know what it had come from, until the lab analyzed it.

Hank recorded the GPS coordinates and radioed Auggie. Grant and Auggie were just reaching the spot where the cross trail intersected the trail they were on. Hank told them to wait there, and he and Cassie would come through to their side.

As they moved away from the intersection, the broken branches diminished as the trail widened. Hank and Cassie walked slowly wanting to make sure they didn't miss any evidence. The trail ran for a hundred yards or so between the two main trails. The vegetation was thick on both sides of the crossover. As Cassie approached the intersection, she spotted the broken branches again at about the same height. Hank explained what they had found on the other end and showed them the hair sample.

Cassie asked if it might be worthwhile to cut off the ends where some of the branches were broken. Even though they couldn't see anything caught in the breaks, the lab might be able to find skin cells or something. It sounded like a good idea, so after Cassie took more photos, everyone pulled out their knives and evidence bags and started cutting off an inch on each broken branch. After they had gathered several, they decided they should head back to camp on their original trails to see if they could spot any other evidence. Sometimes looking at things from a different direction allowed you to see things you had missed when approaching from the opposite direction.

Back at camp, the team was excited that they might have found proof. Any real evidence of Bigfoot would be a huge find. They all told Cassie that they thought her idea about the branches might yield something in the lab. As far as they knew, no one had tried that before.

They all found it a little easier to get to sleep that night. Cassie's head was nestled on Hank's shoulder and the camp was quiet and peaceful until something large hit the side of the tent. Cassie jerked awake and sat up, poking Hank in the ribs to wake him.

"What's wrong?" he asked, still half asleep.

Before Cassie answered, something large hit the other side of the tent hitting Hank in the back.

"What the hell? Cassie, lie down and put your pillow and sleeping bag over your head," he whispered in her ear.

"What's going...," she started to ask, but he put his hand over her mouth to keep her quiet. He put his upper body over her head and pulled his pillow and sleeping bag over them both. Cassie had no idea how long they stayed that way, but at least two more things crashed into the tent. When it had been quiet for a few minutes Hank had to take action. He needed to make sure everyone was OK. He uncovered cautiously and found his flashlight. Cassie followed his lead. They both pulled out weapons and made sure they were loaded and the safeties were off. They crawled from the tent and Hank immediately shined his light on the surrounding tree line. Cassie followed suit. Something big standing upright on two feet ran into the woods, but they didn't get a good look at it. Auggie and Grant came out armed with lights and guns as well. When they looked around the campsite, they saw that there were several large rocks against the tents that hadn't been there earlier.

"Did Bigfoot do this?" Cassie asked.

"Can't say for sure, but likely. It's a behavior they are said to exhibit. Other than a fairly large man, I don't know what else could do this," Hank said.

"Is everyone all right? Did anybody get hit?" he asked.

"Only you, I guess. Are you OK?" Cassie queried.

"I'm fine. Maybe a bruise but nothing serious. I'm thinking we have stumbled into a Bigfoot's territory, and it doesn't want us here," Hank explained.

There was some discussion about what to do next, but they had few options. Hank hoped that they had scared the creature off for the night. They all crawled back into the tents and tried to get back to sleep. They all knew that wasn't likely to happen.

X X X

At first light, they all were up and ready to start the day. No one slept much, and they were all still wired from their encounter.

Cassie photographed the campsite with the rocks, and they investigated the tree line for any evidence but came up empty. The plan had been to spend the morning on the trails and then pack up camp and head back into Santa Fe. They decided they might as well stick with the plan. They found no further evidence and were back in Santa Fe in time for dinner.

"So what happens now," Cassie asked.

"Auggie and Grant will head home tomorrow," Hank replied, "but I think I'm going to stay thru the upcoming weekend just to enjoy New Mexico a bit more." Cassie didn't miss the knowing look that passed between Auggie and Grant. "I'll turn in the evidence we gathered, when I get back to Montana next week, and we'll see if the lab finds anything useful."

Before heading to her room for the night, Cassie told Auggie and Grant how much she appreciated them allowing her to be part of the team, though she would be glad to hear Zuck was back on active duty.

Hank knocked on Cassie's door a little while later. "I thought I should make sure you didn't have any plans for the weekend before I just assumed I should stay."

"I have nothing on my agenda. I'm happy to spend as much time with you as possible," Cassie assured him. "What do you have in mind?" Cassie asked, wondering if they would stay in Santa Fe or head back to Las Cruces.

"Well, I have many things in mind," he said with a bad movie leer, "what would you like to do?"

"Probably many of the same things you have in mind, but the real question is do you want to do them in Santa Fe or head back to Las Cruces?"

"I'd love to see you on your home turf, if that's OK. I don't want to impose, if you want to keep that mystery going a while longer," Hank said.

"No mystery. My condo's a mess, but I think you'll survive the shock. Let's head back to Cruces tomorrow so you can get a taste of the desert. It'll be easier if you change your return flight to El Paso. That way we don't have to get you back to Albuquerque. We can figure out the details either way."

They kissed good night, and Hank headed back to his room for a good night's sleep. Cassie packed up some of her gear and sent Bob a text message that she was heading home in the morning.

Auggie and Grant were gone by the time Cassie and Hank met for breakfast. They ate quickly, packed up their gear, and checked-out.

CHAPTER FORTY-FOUR

Once south of the Albuquerque airport, Cassie switched into tour guide mode. Hank had never been to southern New Mexico. Cassie pointed out the Bosque del Apache Wildlife Refuge, where thousands of photographers line the roads each November to photograph the migrating Sandhill cranes. She told Hank the story of Truth or Consequences, the town named after a television game show. She pointed out the water level lines at Elephant Butte Lake that showed how badly the drought had affected the area. They passed the sign for Spaceport America where they plan to launch commercial spacecraft. It surprised Hank that the border check point on the northbound side of Interstate 25 was located so far from the border. As they approached the north side of Las Cruces, Cassie pointed out the large white radar dishes standing like giant flowers in the desert. The dishes are part of NASA's White Sands Test Facility.

Hank couldn't believe how many interesting things they'd seen just from the interstate. He now understood why Cassie liked living here. It was a really interesting part of the country, but he wasn't so sure about the scenery. You could see for miles, but there wasn't much to see. It felt exposed, and the temperature had risen steadily as they drove south. In the SUV with the AC on high, it was comfortable, but whenever they stopped and got out, it was like opening the door of a blast furnace. Hank couldn't imagine doing much outdoors when it was this hot, but Cassie assured him that the temperature didn't stop her from hiking or rock hounding in the desert. She said it was all about conditioning.

The Organ Mountains' spectacular rocky peaks loomed over the city, as majestic as the Tetons in Wyoming. She exited from the highway and drove to her condo. "You know that if you'd rather stay at a hotel, I won't be offended," Cassie told him. "Well, at least not too much. I only have the one bathroom and there's not much room for you to escape me here."

"Somehow, I don't think I'll mind that at all," Hank said as they unloaded the car.

X X X

Cassie's condo was small but efficient. The large kitchen counter divided the kitchen from the living and dining area. Cassie often used her laptop at the counter to change things up from spending so much time at her desk. She had painted the walls in earth tones except for her bedroom which was painted a deep eggplant purple. All of the walls were decorated with of Cassie's photos of bugs or other desert critters and scenery. Tony always complained that the bug pictures above the bed creeped him out, but Hank didn't comment.

It was after noon, so Cassie suggested they head out for lunch and stock up at the grocery so they could settle in for the rest of the day and make plans for how to spend the next three days. Cassie took him, to her favorite Italian restaurant. They ate and went to the grocery making sure they picked up something to cook for dinner later.

Back at the condo, Cassie unpacked and started laundry while Hank submitted his final report on their investigation at the caldera. Cassie's weapons locker remodel impressed him, and he helped her secure all the firearms back in place. Cassie emailed her Mom that she was home safe and would call to talk soon. She conveniently forgot to mention that Hank had come home with her.

Cassie hoped she wasn't being naive, but it felt perfectly normal to share her space with Hank. Whenever Tony was here, he complained about everything, but Hank seemed at home and settled, even though he'd only been there a few hours. He stood for several minutes studying the grouping of Thunderbird photos on the living room wall.

"I've seen a lot of these photos on the BITES database, but seeing them here, and realizing you took them is pretty amazing."

"Thanks. Sometimes I forget how incredible it is that the Thunderbirds even exist. All of the killing attributed to them makes it hard to be a fan, I guess."

It was a quiet, pleasant evening. They talked about what they'd do the next three days, turned on the SyFy channel, and watched a movie about Bigfoot. It was surreal to watch something like that after having just returned from searching for the creature. Cassie got that strange feeling again of reality not being what she once thought it was.

CHAPTER FORTY-FIVE

Hank wanted Cassie to take him to the desert in search of the Thunderbirds, but they decided to save that for the next day when they would prepare to get a very early start. It would give Hank at least a day to acclimate to the heat. After breakfast, they drove out Highway 70 to White Sands National Monument. The highway cuts right through the missile range and traffic is stopped at certain times due to testing.

White Sands is always fun for visitors. As you drive into the park, the sides of the road are so white it seems like you're driving on snow, but it's a hundred degrees. You can rent saucer sleds at the gift shop and slide down the dunes. At the monument, Hank could experience the desert heat without really being out of reach of help if necessary. Being a seasoned outdoorsman, he wanted to go for the four-mile hike, but Cassie assured him that wasn't a good idea until he was used to the heat and dryness. They opted for a shorter trail of just over a mile. They both carried plenty of water, but by the time they returned to the car, Hank was convinced. He couldn't seem to drink enough water, and his skin was so dry he thought maybe something was physically wrong with him. Cassie laughed at his complaints. "See, the desert will make you tougher," she explained.

Hank wondered about that. Cassie was certainly tough in some respects, but she managed to remain feminine. He fell asleep wondering how she pulled that off. He didn't want to sleep, but he couldn't stop himself. He hated to waste a minute of his time with Cassie, but the heat and dryness took some getting used to. After a shower, they both felt better. Hank had gotten sun burned in spite of applying SPF 50 sunscreen, but it was only a minor irritation. After relaxing for a bit and re-hydrating, they went out for a big dinner. Hank admitted the desert demanded respect much like that required to undertake an outdoor activity in arctic locales.

X X X

Cassie had prepped their packs for the outing with plenty of sunscreen, extra water, hats, and overshirts to cut down on the risk of Hank getting more sun burned. They picked up breakfast bagels and drove out to Rabbit Ears pass. They always had a good time hiking together, but today was special for Cassie because she was introducing Hank to her world. She loved the desert, and although she had enjoyed her recent experience in the mountains and forests of the northwest, this was where she felt at home.

They hadn't talked much about Cassie's entomology degree, but Hank got to see that side of her too, when they found a vinegaroon on the trail. Cassie explained that though vinegaroons are one of the most frightening looking bugs in the southwest, they're harmless to humans. If threatened, they release an odor that smells like vinegar. Cassie impressed Hank even more. Here she was fascinated by a creature that most women would run away from screaming.

Cassie made sure Hank drank plenty of water and reapplied his sunscreen every couple of hours. They made good progress. She took him to the area where she had found the first tracks of the Thunderbirds. Hank asked how that happened, and Cassie decided she was ready to share the details of her abduction with him. As they continued hiking, she told him the story from beginning to end. It shocked him that she could relate the events so dispassionately. "Cassie, are you sure you're OK being out here again after what happened?"

"I've been out here many times since then. It's not a problem," she assured him.

"You are a wonder, Ms. Carter," Hank said. "I found you so impressive before today, but after knowing what all has happened to you in the past few months and seeing you in your element, I can't imagine there being a more amazing woman."

"Thanks, Hank. I'm certainly glad that's how you feel, but it's just who I am. In case you haven't realized it already, I find you pretty interesting yourself," Cassie told him, stopping to give him a hug. As they continued walking, Cassie tried to quantify what it was about Hank that she found so appealing. Nice looking, muscular, caring, and authoritative were the first words that came to mind. None of those seemed to justify her feelings for him.

Shrugging out of her pack, Cassie said, "From here on, we need to be alert, just like when you're on a field op for BITES. This is the Thunderbirds' territory. They've never acted at all aggressively when I've seen them, but knowing they've been responsible for several deaths, we should be extremely cautious." Cassie opened her backpack, took out a dart gun, and put it in the pocket of her cargo pants. "You should get the pistol out of your pack just in case." Hank hadn't realized she'd packed weapons. It surprised him how quickly she went from easygoing hiker to armed federal agent.

They stopped every few minutes and checked the distant ridgeline but saw nothing. Cassie had led them on a path near where she found the nest and Marina. It was likely that at least one of the birds frequented the area. Suddenly she put her hand up in a closed fist to signal a stop. Hank looked at her, and she pointed to the northeast. She looked through the binoculars and could see a Thunderbird heading toward the nest. She passed the binoculars to him. His gasp told her he'd spotted it. Cassie whispered she was going to move closer. They circled around behind the rock formation sheltering the nest and climbed to the top to get a better view. The bird was several yards away but headed in their direction. Cassie took photos while Hank watched. They both tensed when the bird stopped and sniffed the air. When it turned and headed back the way it had come, they both released the breath they'd been holding. They moved down the rocks and started back, keeping a close eye on the bird.

When they were out of earshot, Hank said, "That was incredible. I can't get over the sheer size of it. I had seen pictures, but nothing prepares you for seeing it in person. It's always that way with cryptids." Adrenalin kept them going all the way to the SUV.

"I've been hunting cryptids for years, and I've never gotten that close to anything that big, that was terrifying, exhilarating, and surreal all at once," Hank said. "Thank you so much for sharing it with me. It was amazing."

"I'm glad you got to see them, but I'm surprised a bit by your reaction," Cassie said. "I thought this was kind of old hat for you. You know, seen one cryptid, seen them all." They both laughed.

When the adrenalin waned, they were exhausted. They had hiked nearly ten miles, and it had been one hundred degrees out. Back at Cassie's, they sat down on the sofa and fell asleep.

Cassie awoke with her head in Hank's lap. He was still sleeping. The sun was just setting, and she was getting hungry.

She ordered pizza and checked out the new pictures they'd taken until Hank woke up a few minutes later.

"Pizza's on its way. Hope pepperoni's OK with you," she said.

"Sounds great," Hank said as he stood and stretched.

When Cassie checked her email before going to bed later that night, she was surprised to find a message from Mr. Meecham. She noticed he had copied Hank and Jim Lansing. The message said local authorities in Las Cruces had asked BITES to track and eradicate the Thunderbirds. This was now an active op, and Cassie was to coordinate with Jim and her team. The "kicker" in the message was that Mr. Meecham knew that Hank was still in New Mexico and asked him to join Jim's team for the operation. Cassie emailed Jim asking what time the team would be arriving in Las Cruces and what, if any, preparations she could assist with. Hank was just getting into bed when she walked in. "You'd better check your email before we turn in," she said.

"Why, is something wrong?" Hank asked. "Is Zuck OK?"

"Everything's fine. Seems you may be sticking around Las Cruces a bit longer than you expected," Cassie said.

Hank checked email on his smart phone and read the message from Mr. Meecham. "I just can't seem to stay away from you no matter how hard I try," he joked as he climbed into bed next to her. "Sounds like we're going on another op together."

X X X

Cassie's morning email check told her Jim, and the rest of the team, would be arriving in El Paso that afternoon and would be in Cruces by 3:00 PM. They had reserved rooms at a local hotel. Jim asked her to meet them there.

"So how are we going to play the room thing?" Cassie asked Hank over breakfast. "Will you get a room at the hotel, too?"

"I think that's best. Especially since this is your first time meeting your team," Hank answered. "I don't want to make the situation any more stressful for you."

"I do like having you here," Cassie told Hank. "But you're right, we need to stick to our plan about keeping our private life separate from BITES."

CHAPTER FORTY-SIX

They waited in the lobby of the hotel for Cassie's team to arrive. Hank had checked into a room and moved in his luggage. He and Cassie agreed that, when this op was concluded he'd try to extend his stay a few days so they could have more time together. This was becoming a habit, and they both were getting used to being together. Cassie worried that it was going to be much harder when they had to part company again once the thunderbird op ended. She knew they'd been lucky to get to spend so much time together.

When the team arrived, Cassie introduced herself and Hank. Once everyone had a chance to wash up and unpack, they met in a hotel meeting room to discuss the op. Since Cassie was the expert on both the Thunderbirds and the area, Jim asked her to handle the briefing. It felt a little weird to her because they all had a lot more experience with BITES that she did, but she was quickly catching up.

When she showed them photos of the birds, they were surprised at the size and the fact that three of the creatures had been documented. None of them had ever been involved in an op with multiple targets. Hank explained it was rare for them to see even one of the cryptids they were hunting. Cassie briefed them on the attacks and the hikers who'd been killed. Hank interjected that he'd been able to see one of the birds himself, and he provided his take on the creatures. Cassie wasn't sure how she felt about that. She understood he was trying to help but worried that someone might figure out that it meant Hank had been in the area before the investigation was activated. Oh well, she had bigger things to worry about for the next few days. Pat was an avowed desert rat like Cassie, but Jim and Garret both had limited desert experience, so Cassie needed to make sure they took adequate precautions.

Jim took over the planning phase of the discussion. "Mr. Meecham told me that we could dispense with the standard interview portion since Cassie, and now I guess even Hank, have spotted the creatures themselves. Unlike our usual ops, we aren't setting out to prove these creatures exist. Cassie has done that for us, so we'll be starting with tracking and eradication. "Cassie, I have to ask, these things are your discovery. Will you have any qualms about taking them out, if need be?"

"I can appreciate your concern," Cassie assured him, "but I've seen the bodies of the hikers. I'll be ready to do what's necessary to eradicate the threat the thunderbirds pose."

"That's good to hear," Jim told her. "Let's plan to head out first thing in the morning. I'm assuming we don't need to map out a route."

Cassie reminded them that it would be very hot the next day. Rattlesnakes posed a serious threat, and they would need to use caution. Lots of water and sunscreen would be required. She asked if they planned to camp in the desert or return to the hotel at night. Jim said they'd plan to return to the hotel for now, but if they determined they needed to go deeper into the desert, they might rethink that after a couple of days.

It had been a long travel day for both Jim and Garrett, so they wanted to get a good night's sleep in preparation for the next day. Cassie and Hank offered to pick up the supplies since they knew the city. They said their goodbyes and the team went their separate ways.

They were able to shop for the supplies and go back to Cassie's to pack up the weapons, before heading out to eat. Over dinner, Hank told her, "When you were out getting the pictures,

Jim took me aside and asked how you did in the field. He knew you joined my team during your training and then again in northern New Mexico. "I had to be honest with him."

"What did you tell him?" Cassie asked with a look of concern on her face.

"I told him there was no agent I'd rather have on a field op and that includes my own team members," Hank grinned. "It seems the story of the shot that brought down the bear and saved Zuck has already made the rounds of BITES. I'm afraid you are legendary, Ms. Carter. If they had any doubts, I could tell them about some of your other talents."

Relieved, she punched him playfully in the shoulder. She still wasn't sure why everyone made such a big deal about her darting the bear. "Do you think he's concerned about having a female on his team?"

"Honestly, I think he's uncertain how it will affect the team, but I suspect he'll be over it quickly, once he's seen you in action," Hank said proudly. "He'll soon be just another member in the vast and quickly growing Cassie Carter fan club, of which, I am the founding member and president, of course."

It was a fun evening, but they knew the next day in the desert would be a tough one whether they encountered the birds or not. After dinner, Cassie dropped Hank off at the hotel and headed back to her condo.

She talked with her Mom and caught her up on things which led, inevitably, to her relationship with Hank. She shared most things with her Mom and wasn't at all good at keeping secrets from her, so it wasn't surprising that her Mom surmised Hank had become much more than a passing fancy. "I wish we were there to meet him," her Mom said. "If you get the chance, introduce him to Bob, he'll be our proxy reviewer." Cassie promised to do just that, if she got a chance.

CHAPTER FORTY-SEVEN

Cassie got up early so she'd have time to load up all her gear as well as all the weapons in her arsenal, since the agents who flew in only brought one weapon each. The team was assembled and ready to go when she got to the hotel. Hank rode with Cassie, and her teammates followed in their rental SUV. Cassie led them to the end of the dirt road closest to the nest area.

She had notified Cory that the BITES team was on site and would be in the desert hunting the birds starting today. She asked that he keep the regular BLM ranger patrols out of the area where she planned to concentrate the search. Everyone geared up, loaded their weapons, and followed Cassie. It was early but already quite warm with bright sunshine. The men traded stories of their work with BITES while Cassie led them toward the nest. She called a halt when they reached the edge of the thunderbirds' territory. It was another hour of hiking to reach the nest, so they needed to maintain silence from that point on. They stopped frequently to scan the area with binoculars for any sign of the birds.

Cassie's plan was to take them to the nest area the first day. It had been the most reliable sighting spot. She didn't expect they'd see all three Thunderbirds but hoped they would find at least one. Once they dealt with the bird that nested there, she would move the search a little further north where the three birds were spotted together.

They would try to capture one of the specimens alive, if at all possible. Mr. Meecham wanted to be able to determine whether these birds were natural or the result of some genetic manipulation or mutation from environmental causes.

Unconvinced that they had a solid plan to incapacitate the birds for transport, Cassie deferred to her fellow agents who had much more experience in that part of the operation.

When they reached the nest area, each of the team members settled in to scan the desert around the nest and raise the alarm if the target was sighted. After an hour of sitting, Cassie decided she wanted to be more proactive, so she headed farther to the north where they'd seen the bird before. Hank went with her. They walked for twenty minutes then stopped and surveyed the arroyo. Sure enough, Cassie spotted the bird headed in the direction of the nest. Hank verified her sighting, and they moved back to the others as quickly as possible, to warn them that the bird was headed their way.

Cassie took the large dart gun and climbed the ridge behind the nest which gave her a great vantage point. Hank was also on the backside of the rocks but a little north of Cassie's position. Jim, Pat, and Garret planned to form a loose circle around the bird and tighten the perimeter until the bird was surrounded and everyone had a shot. As the bird approached, Hank saw that it carried something in its mouth, but he couldn't tell what. The bird went to the nest, dropped whatever it was carrying, and moved some of the nesting material around as though trying to cover up its prize. When it was satisfied, it turned to head back up the arroyo.

As the bird turned, Cassie had a perfect shot at its neck, and she took it. The Thunderbird was much larger than the bear that attacked Zuck. It reacted to the sting of the dart, but it was not immobilized. It started to move north again. Cassie reloaded and placed another shot squarely between its shoulder blades. It let out a squeal but still didn't go down. The team saw that the animal was not succumbing to the sedative, so Jim gave the order for everyone to fire. Cassie pulled out her pistol, and everyone fired on the giant bird. There were some misses but plenty of hits. Eventually the bird keeled over. Cassie and Hank verified it was dead before motioning for the rest of the team to approach.

"Clearly we need to find a more potent load for the dart gun for something this large," Jim said. "Good shooting, Cassie."

Cassie looked at the Thunderbird closer than she had ever been able to before. It was magnificent. She had never seen one fly and wasn't sure if they could or not, but their immense size was impressive. Examining it up close, it was obvious that the claws and beak were powerful enough to rip apart a human being. Hank and Cassie volunteered to stay with the body while Jim, Pat, and Garrett hiked out far enough to get cell service so they could call Mr. Meecham to arrange an immediate chopper pick up. Cassie and Hank would hike out after transport removed the body. They'd meet the team back at the hotel. While they waited for the chopper to arrive, Cassie photographed the bird from every conceivable angle. Then she and Hank sat on the rocks looking at the amazing bird and waiting.

When the chopper arrived, stirring up all the nesting materials, they lowered a couple of men who helped Hank and Cassie secured straps and harnesses around the carcass. They worried that the cables might not be able to lift the bird. It was much larger than they expected. The four of them struggled to get the cables around the bird's body. Once secured, the chopper lifted the bird very slowly and headed off. When the chopper flew away, Cassie and Hank gathered up their gear and prepared for the long walk back to the SUV.

Before they left the area, Hank checked the nest to see if he could locate what the bird had dropped off. Unfortunately, he succeeded. He found a human arm. They had no way of knowing whether it was from one of the already known victims or someone else. They needed to take it with them, though the thought of that caused Cassie to shiver. They both had extra shirts in their packs so they wrapped the arm as best they could, transferred all of Hanks gear into Cassie's pack, and placed the arm in Hank's backpack for the journey back to town.

CHAPTER FORTY-EIGHT

Back in Las Cruces, Hank and Cassie stopped at the police station to turn in the arm. They explained where and how they'd found it. The detective who took their statements said he'd contact them once they determined if it belonged to a known victim. Cassie and Hank both felt the need to wash up before leaving the station. At Cassie's, Hank relaxed while she took a quick shower before they headed back to the hotel. Cassie waited in Hank's room while he got cleaned up, and then they went to meet the team in Jim's room. Everyone was pretty stoked from their encounter with the Thunderbird. They were discussing reports that needed to be made and different strategies for locating and eradicating the remainder of the birds. Hank said, "I wanted to give you an update. After the helicopter removed the carcass, I took a look around the nest. I wondered about what the bird had dropped before we shot it. I found a human arm. Cassie and I packed it up and took it to the police station. They'll let us know if this is from one of the victims they already knew about or a new body."

"Sorry to hear that but better that you found it than some unsuspecting hiker. I'll leave it to you two to report on the transport and finding the arm, since the rest of us weren't involved," Jim said, nodding at Hank and Cassie. "Let's talk about what we can do to deal with the immense size of these birds. It's clear our standard methods and weapons are insufficient."

The group threw out some ideas but came up with no obvious solutions. Jim suggested they all retreat to their rooms for some R&R and to file their reports on the day's activities. Cassie retrieved her laptop from the SUV and crashed in Hank's room. After emailing the reports, they had some time to relax before dinner.

The team walked over to the restaurant next door to the hotel and took a large corner booth, so they could eat and discuss ways of dealing with the size problem. Cassie asked if BITES ever called on the military for assistance. There was Holloman Air Force Base in Alamogordo, and Fort Bliss in El Paso. Maybe they would have ideas on how to deal with the large creatures. Hank said he'd coordinated with the Marines once during a search but wasn't sure what the official protocol was. Cassie also suggested that it might be helpful to involve Bob in their discussions. He was a seasoned BLM ranger and was almost as familiar with the birds and the area as Cassie was.

It was decided that the next day would be spent coming up with a plan and making necessary adjustments to weapons and equipment. Back in Hank's room, Cassie called Bob and asked him to meet with the team the next morning. He was excited to help and especially interested in meeting "this Hank" he'd heard so much about.

Hank called Mr. Meecham and explained the challenges they had bringing down the giant bird and securing it for transport. Meecham said he'd make some calls and military resources would meet with them at 9:00 AM the next morning. Cassie called the front desk and reserved a meeting room for the next day so they'd have space for everyone.

X X X

Cassie introduced Bob to the team, and just after 9:00 AM, representatives from the Air Force, the Army, and the National Guard arrived. Since the military was new to the operation, Jim asked Cassie to provide an overview of the birds and pass around the pictures. When she finished, there were some questions. Not surprisingly, the Air Force contingent asked if the bird could fly. "We aren't sure. No one has reported seeing them fly. If we assume the Thunderbird has maintained some similarity to a standard sized bird species then it may be capable of flight but, with its size, probably only for short distances," Cassie explained.

Jim took over and provided details about the operation the previous day and the challenges they'd encountered due to the animals large size.

"So," Jim continued, "there are at least two more of these birds out there that we need to capture or kill. The preference is take at least one alive, if it's possible to do so safely. Let's start with figuring out what we can do to incapacitate the creatures."

Bob asked if a local doctor or vet could load the darts with a stronger, more potent sedative. There seemed to be no issue with the darts piercing the bird's skin, but the dosage wasn't sufficient for the bird's body mass. They all agreed that they'd have to do this to have any hope of incapacitating the birds.

Next, they discussed ammunition. It had taken several shots from the five BITES' agents to drop the bird. The Rangers decided everyone should switch to guns that could use .50 caliber rounds in hopes that it would take less hits to bring down the remaining birds. The Army offered to have some Rangers join the team. They would be armed with RPGs which would fell the creature immediately. Although it sounded extreme to Cassie, the team agreed that it would be a prudent option to have at their disposal.

Everyone agreed that cables would be best for securing the creature once it was incapacitated. The Army said they could provide enough cable for the operation. By noon, everyone had their assignments and the meeting adjourned. The hunt team would meet in the morning at 5:00 AM at the National Guard Armory. They would be taking military vehicles into the search area.

After the meeting broke-up, Cassie found Bob talking with Hank in the lobby. "Thanks for your help getting the sedative, Bob." Cassie said, joining them. "Will you be going with us tomorrow?"

"Looks like you'll have plenty of manpower, so I'll let you young people handle it," Bob replied.

"How are you feeling about us having to capture or kill the Thunderbirds?" Cassie asked, laying her hand in Bob's forearm.

"OK. We've seen what can happen when these birds interact with humans. It's sad, but they can't be allowed to roam free or no one would be safe in the desert."

The BITES team had lunch together and reviewed the plans. Cassie and Hank would pick up the super-strength tranquilizer when it was ready. Bob had worked with the FWS team to have a local veterinarian prepare the necessary dosages. Jim would file a report with Mr. Meecham detailing the military's involvement. This had now become a much larger operation than BITES was normally involved with, so they wanted to make sure everything was documented. Pat and Garrett would pick up provisions for the BITES team.

After lunch, everyone went their separate ways. Hank and Cassie found themselves alone again. Even when they didn't plan it, fate seemed to keep pushing them together. Hank knew he was in love with her, but found it odd that although he could easily think of her as his girlfriend and see her in that role, she was also turning out to be a great field agent and someone he enjoyed working with. He found the dichotomy weird when he stopped to think about it. Fortunately, during an active op, there was little time for thinking about much of anything but the op.

Hank and Cassie headed to her condo to relax and wait for the call from Bob letting them know the sedative was ready for pickup. "Is this level of chaos normal in a field op?" Cassie asked as they settled in on the sofa with their coffee.

"Not really," Hank answered, "but it seems to be happening more since you've been involved," he teased her. When he saw that she wasn't laughing, he explained. "In my time at BITES, I've never been involved in an op where we had to call in the military. These creatures are much larger than anything I've dealt with. That fact, coupled with the fact that we have multiple birds to deal with, has complicated this operation considerably. Add to those things the fact that some of the bird's habitat might be located on White Sands Missile Range, and we've got a pretty complex situation."

They watched a movie and tried to relax until the call came in that they could pick up the tranquilizer. They picked up the sedative and drove back to the hotel to pack it for transport. There were messages waiting for them from Jim, saying the team would be relaxing in the bar next door, if they wanted to join them. It was really the first chance they'd had to get acquainted with Cassie's teammates. Pat Murphy was Irish through and through--the accent, the jokes, the Guinness. Garrett was the quiet one of the team. Jim seemed nice enough and had proven a capable leader thus far, but something about his "good ol' boy" manner rubbed Cassie the wrong way. She was sure they could work together with no problem, but she doubted they'd ever become friends. Cassie considered herself adaptable, but she'd have to ask Hank how one moved to another team in BITES. She wouldn't want to make any move soon, but long term, it was something she might need to know.

As seemed to be the norm for BITES teams, most of their camaraderie was centered on their past investigations. Though Cassie didn't have many ops to draw from, she certainly had been part of some of the most exciting.

She asked them to describe how their BITES training was done, wondering how things had changed over time. Pat went through training with two other agents, and it sounded like the training covered all the same things as Cassie had covered in her recent training. Garrett admitted that his training lasted six weeks because he had difficulties with some of the weapons training and had to spend extra time. Jim had gone through BITES training five years ago. He was one of the first field agents to get the structured training. He admitted that at the time, he hated the computer part of it, but now he realized how large a part that played in what they did. It was a pleasant evening. The group ordered food in the bar and headed back to the hotel early. They knew the next day was going to be long and stressful.

CHAPTER FORTY-NINE

At sunrise, all those participating in the hunt met at the armory and loaded into military Humvees with National Guard drivers. As a final option, an Air Force officer accompanied them. He would call in an air strike, if required, to take out the Thunderbirds. Cassie felt a little odd. She was used to being the only female or one of very few, that wasn't the issue, but this looked like an assault force. She looked at Garrett's face and could tell that he felt even more out of place than she did. They bounced along the road in silence until they reached the coordinates Cassie provided which were at the southwestern edge of the known territory of the birds. The vehicles stopped and everyone disembarked. The drivers would stay with the vehicles. The rest of the team loaded their weapons, shouldered their packs, and followed Cassie. With all the various organizations involved, it was hard to tell who was in charge, but it was obvious who was leading the team, and that was Cassie. It made sense, but it still felt strange when she looked over her shoulder at the line of armed soldiers snaking off into the desert behind her.

The plan was simple--spot one of the giant birds, surround it, and incapacitate it with tranquilizers. If that didn't work, they would take it down with bullets. If that failed, the Army Rangers would be called in. If they still hadn't been successful in downing the bird, the Air Force Colonel would radio for an air strike. Regardless of how they stopped the bird, once it was down, it would be secured with cables, and a helicopter would be called to transport the creature, sedated or dead, to the BITES lab.

Cassie led the way to the series of rocky ridges where she had photographed the three birds together. She called a halt at the base of the first ridgeline and explained that they were in the most likely area to spot the Thunderbirds. Hank suggested they fan out along the ridge, so they would get a broader view. Everyone had been issued binoculars and knew what to look for. They climbed the ridge and stopped at the peak to scout the desert below and in front of them. No one detected any movement. They planned to climb up and down each ridge just like Cassie had Bob had done several weeks before, stopping at the top of each ridge to survey the area for signs of the giant birds.

Cassie gained a new appreciation for the military as she experienced first-hand how difficult it was to move even a group this small in any sort of coordinated formation. By afternoon, they had reached the top of the third ridge. Surveying the desert and arroyos below, one of the soldiers spotted movement far to the northeast. Cassie joined the soldier and trained her binoculars on the area he pointed out. She saw a thunderbird. It was still a long way off. Jim and Hank discussed the options and decided they would hold their position until the bird had passed by, and then they would move out and surround it from behind.

They all kept their binoculars trained on the bird until it came close enough to be visible to the naked eye. Those seeing the bird for the first time were stunned by the size. It was so quiet you could almost hear the giant bird breathing as it passed their location. When it was still in view, but well south of their position, Jim gave the signal to move out. The team moved across the valley floor as quickly and quietly as possible. Cassie positioned herself on the east side of the circle where she would have a direct shot at the neck of the bird. Pat was on the opposite side hoping to make the same shot as Cassie.

As they tightened the ring around the bird, it started to freak out. It flapped its wings and made lots of clicking noises. The massive beak snapped together with a loud crack that reminded them all to keep their distance. Unfortunately, they had surrounded the bird in the open desert leaving all the hunters completely exposed.

Cassie got antsy to take the shot. She wanted to slow the thing down, but was supposed to wait for a signal from Jim. Finally, the signal came, and she took the shot, hitting the bird in the side of its neck. Pat fired at the same time but missed and fired twice more before hitting the bird on the shoulder. The Thunderbird took a step and wobbled a bit, then took another step. The soldiers moved back slightly to give the bird room to move a little. Cassie had reloaded, and her next shot hit the bird in the center of its breast. The bird turned looking for the source of the new pain, but it looked at them with glassy eyes. It took a step toward Cassie before falling over on its side, while soldiers scrambled out of the way.

At the same time, Cassie's shot hit the bird in its breast, it screeched, and another Thunderbird appeared running toward the attack. No one had anticipated that.

The second bird took flight and Cassie understood where the name came from. The sound its wings made was deafening. The bird landed inside the circle of hunters next to the injured bird. It flew so low that its claws injured two soldiers as it passed over their heads. Three men got trapped under the first bird when it fell. They had been distracted by the second bird and hadn't gotten out of the way quickly enough. Hank yelled to Cassie to shoot the second bird. She reloaded and took aim, but she was too close to hit the neck so she settled for a chest shot. It had no immediate effect.

Most of the team was busy aiding the injured men and trying to extricate those trapped under the fallen bird. Hank and Cassie seemed to be the only two focused on the second bird. It was still standing, flapping its huge wings, and clicking. Cassie reloaded and was preparing for another shot when the bird flew off. It flew only a few feet off the ground and landed about forty yards away then took off running. Cassie looked to Hank for guidance. "Let's take care of the situation here. There's no way we can catch that one right now," he said.

Cassie checked on the downed bird and injected more sedation. With all of them working together, they lifted the bird sufficiently to allow them to pull the trapped men free. They moved all the injured a safe distance away from the Thunderbird and evaluated their conditions. Most had only minor scrapes and bruises, a few would need stitches, and two of the men trapped by the fallen creature probably had cracked ribs and could have some broken bones or internal injuries. They stabilized the injured and called a medical transport helicopter.

Everyone who wasn't involved in tending to the injured, assisted in securing the fallen bird. Cassie took photographs, while they waited for the helicopters to arrive. The BITES team remained with the creature awaiting transport. The rest of the group started the long hike back to the Humvees so they could get those with minor injuries to medical care as quickly as possible. While they waited, Jim said he thought their plan had been good except that they had failed to consider the possibility of one of the birds coming to the aid of another.

"As far as we know, there is only one of these giant birds left out here," Jim said. "I think we can just resupply and follow the same plan tomorrow. Cassie, you decide where we should start the search. You've been dead on so far."

Cassie happily let Jim take the lead on the long hike back to the vehicles. The combination of heat, hiking, and the adrenaline rush subsiding, left them all exhausted by the time the Humvee came into view. Their driver tried to make small talk, asking about the bird and the attack, but they were all too tired to offer more than an occasional grunt in reply. The guys all rode back to the hotel to file reports and crash, leaving Cassie alone. She took a hot shower, made some coffee, and prepared her report. As soon as she hit the send button submitting her report to BITES, she was falling asleep. She set her alarm to wake her in two hours. She wanted to eat dinner and call Hank before calling it a night.

CHAPTER FIFTY

Mr. Meecham emailed congratulations to the team on capturing the Thunderbird specimen alive. Cassie had some emails about upcoming shooting competitions which reminded her she hadn't been able to practice for several days, but she'd get back to it when she could. Just as she was starting to think about what she could make for dinner, Hank called and asked if she wanted to pick him up and grab something to eat.

X X X

"So how are you doing with all of this?" Hank asked after they'd ordered.

"OK, I think," Cassie said tentatively. "Trying to come to grips with this whirlwind that has become my life lately."

"You're doing great," Hank told her. "I don't want it to overwhelm you. The ops we've been involved with recently have been extreme and unusual in a number of ways. This isn't typical of BITES. I hope the intensity level doesn't make you rethink your decision to join the agency."

"Thanks, I appreciate your concern," Cassie told him. "I'll let you know if I feel like I'm losing it."

"In spite of what you think, this has been a successful op so far," Hank assured her.

"Well, perhaps the streak will continue, and we'll be able to find the last Thunderbird tomorrow and wrap this thing up. I wanted to ask you, will we shut down the op once the third bird is found? We don't know if there are more of them out there."

"Thanks to you, we know there are three, so unless we find evidence of more, I expect we'll close this one out, once the third bird is captured," Hank explained.

"I guess we never know how many of the creatures we hunt are out there, do we?" Cassie realized.

X X X

They met back at the armory at oh-dark-thirty, ready for the hunt. The military folks reported that all of those injured had been released from the hospital with the exception of one soldier with some broken bones and a collapsed lung, and he was expected to make a full recovery. New soldiers replaced the injured and an additional squad of National Guardsmen joined the group to increase their overall numbers. Everyone was hoping for a day with no surprises.

Later that morning, Cassie found herself trekking through the desert again loaded down with weapons with a trail of armed soldiers at her back. She had learned that life can get really weird very quickly. She shook her head as she thought about her current circumstance. Here she was armed to the teeth leading a group of soldiers into the desert for the purpose of killing a species she'd discovered. And if that wasn't weird enough, one of those men following her was someone she hoped would be a part of her life for a very long time to come.

Walking due east in the morning, the sun had been blinding, making it difficult to spot anything in that direction, but as the day wore on, the route turned to the north and visibility increased. Because of the challenge of keeping everyone moving at a similar pace and the need to cover such a large area of the desert, Cassie suggested to Jim that they try employing the old western approach of sending out scouts. They asked for volunteers and sent out four pairs of scouts, one in each compass point direction. The pairs could move faster than the main group. They would radio in if they spotted anything. Removing the eight men from the main group had the added benefit of making it smaller so even the larger group moved a little quicker. Cassie wanted to be on one of the scout teams, but she was needed to lead the larger group, so she had to move slower than she liked.

They walked and looked, and looked and walked but saw nothing of interest.

"Maybe you've used up all of your beginner's luck," Jim said. "This is what cryptid hunting is normally like--hours and hours with no results."

Cassie wasn't sure why he was being so negative, but she saw no reason to respond. Everyone was getting restless. The first two days had yielded two Thunderbirds, so everyone expected they were easy to find. Cassie knew better, but even she had hoped they'd find the third bird quickly. They didn't.

Jim called a halt mid-afternoon and announced they needed to head back to the vehicles. He radioed the scout teams and passed along the message. Cassie and Hank both overheard Jim's radio call when he said "Seems our little princess has come up empty today." Hank expected he might have to physically restrain Cassie she was so upset, but she bit her tongue and said nothing. The group still hoped to find the bird on their return trip, but they saw only rocks and cactus.

As they made their way back to the vehicles, Cassie realized it had gotten a lot darker. It was too early for the monsoon season in southern New Mexico, but sometimes storms popped up with no regard to the calendar. Though rare this time of year, storms could drop a significant amount of rain in a very short time flooding arroyos and roads. The chance for high winds, hail, dramatic temperature shifts, and a high number of lightning strikes was unlikely but not unheard of.

The wind picked up and the swirling sand made it difficult to see obstacles, so they had to slow down. Cassie heard thunder in the distance. It looked like a major storm, but you could never really tell. The thunder might rumble. There'd be a temperature drop. Maybe they'd even see some flashes of lightning, and then that might be it. They might never see one drop of rain. On the other hand they could see over an inch of rain in just a few minutes. If the legends were to be believed, it was all because someone made the Thunderbirds angry. If there was any truth to those legends, they could be in for a big storm.

The number of men in the open desert carrying all sorts of weapons and electronic equipment worried her. Thankfully, they were close to the mine where the BLM rangers stashed emergency supplies. Though Cassie had been back in the area several times since her abduction, this would be the first time since then she'd been to the mine. She didn't even think about that until later. They needed shelter. There really wasn't any option. She radioed that based on the sky she thought they should go for shelter which was about ten minutes away and ride out the storm if necessary.

Cassie led them to the mine as quickly as possible. The rain started just before the first men reached the tunnels. The sky crackled with so much electricity it sounded like popcorn popping. There was almost no real shelter in the desert. It was just a stroke of luck that they were close to the old mine when the storm hit.

Cassie led them down the tunnels far enough to get everyone out of harm's way. They had enough space to sit and rest while they waited. Once everyone was inside, Hank made his way through the group to find Cassie.

"Cass, are you OK?" Hank asked

"Sure. We'll just have to sit tight here until the storm passes. It's just not safe to keep everyone out in the open when this place was so close," she answered.

"It was good that we could utilize the shelter, but isn't this where you tried to escape when you were abducted?"

"Yes, but I'm fine. Please don't make a big deal out of it."

He whispered in her ear, "I wish I could hold you right now."

She whispered back. "That's completely inappropriate, but thanks for your concern. I'm really fine."

The men closest to the mine entrance kept tabs on the storm, and the others relaxed as best they could. The rain was intense but only lasted for a few minutes.

Cassie went outside and looked around. There had been some significant rain, but it had already soaked into the dry desert soil. They might encounter some mud, but it would be minimal. The storm had moved off in the direction opposite where they needed to go, so Cassie sounded the all clear and got the group moving again.

CHAPTER FIFTY-ONE

On the drive back to town, Cassie asked Jim what the plan was for the following day. "I'm not really sure. You're the expert. Why don't you figure it out," he snapped.

Cassie noticed Hank turn around and look at her from the front seat. "That's fine," she answered. "I'll have a plan together for morning. I assume you, Pat, and Garrett can handle resupply duties so I'm free to concentrate on the plan."

"Um, well yeah, I guess so," Jim stammered, clearly caught off guard by Cassie's quick acceptance of the assignment.

X X X

When they got back to the armory, Hank whispered to Cassie, "Follow my lead. Jim, I'm going to drop Cassie off so I can borrow her car tonight. I'm meeting some friends for dinner and don't want you guys to be stuck at the hotel since you need to get the supplies. Is that OK with you Cassie?"

"Sure thing," Cassie said. "I've got a full night of planning ahead, so I'm not going anywhere. Can you pick me up in the morning?"

"No problem," Hank said with a wink only Cassie could see.

Alone in Cassie's SUV, both she and Hank broke out laughing. "Well played sir," Cassie said, giving Hank a high-five. "What's your real plan? I really do need to make a plan for tomorrow's op."

"I know," Hank assured her, "I think we can accomplish that and fit in a little fun too."

Hank dropped Cassie off at home and stopped by the hotel to pick up some of his things. He saw no reason to continue humoring Jim or worrying about what he thought. Jim had stepped over the line in his treatment of Cassie, and Hank considered that grossly unprofessional.

Cassie answered her door to find Hank carrying his duffel bag and Chinese takeout. "So what happened, did your friends cancel on you?" she teased.

"No, in fact, we're having Chinese takeout right here."

"Listen, Hank, Jim's my team leader, and I don't want to piss him off, but his actions are over the line. I do intend to make a plan for tomorrow. I'd appreciate your help and input, but I'll understand if you feel it's inappropriate for you to help me."

"Oh no, I'm helping you any way I can. Jim is not behaving appropriately for a BITES team leader. What can I do to help?"

It was clear that they had found the nest of only one of the three birds they had seen, so one way to approach the search would be to locate likely nesting areas. These would be sheltered and not out in the open desert. That limited the places to look. Cassie explained her idea to Hank. He thought it made good sense. They could expect to find two more nests and one of them should be the one used by the last of the birds.

"Is there a way we can do the bulk of the search for the nests using ATV's or mountain bikes?" Cassie asked. "It would allow us to cover the area more quickly. There's going to be a lot of open desert between the possible nesting sites. It would mean splitting up the team, but it might be the best option."

"Sounds like a sensible plan to me," Hank agreed. "I'll go call Capt. Barber and Lt. Gold to see if either the Army or National Guard has any ATVs we can borrow."

Hank went into the bedroom to make his calls, while Cassie served up the Chinese food. "Ten M-Gators will be waiting for us at the armory in the morning courtesy of the US Army," Hank said sitting down at the bar. "We'll have them for the next few days if we need them."

While they ate, Cassie explained how she planned to deploy the ten teams of two. After they packed the leftover cartons of food in the fridge, she laid out her plan, showing Hank the assigned areas on a topo map she had spread out on the table. They finalized their plans and then both took some time to do emails and submit their reports on the day's op. "Have you heard how Zuck's doing?" Cassie asked as they were both working on their laptops, Cassie at the desk and Hank at kitchen counter.

"I just got an email from him today saying he thinks he's ready to go back in the field," Hank relayed. "He asked me to talk to Meecham and find out how we make that happen, so I sent an email. At this point, I suspect we'll include Zuck in our next field op, but keep a close eye on him to make sure he really is OK."

"That's good news," Cassie said sincerely. "I'm glad he's getting over it."

"I doubt he'll ever get over the fact that a kick-ass chick with a really big gun saved his life," Hank said, laughing, "But his other wounds seem to have healed."

After they shut down their laptops for the night and prepared their gear for morning, Hank asked Cassie what she thought of her new team. "Don't let this go to your head or anything, but I'd much rather be on your team," she said. "Your guys didn't treat me any different or hassle me because I'm a female. Pat and Garrett don't seem to have a problem with it, but Jim's another story."

CHAPTER FIFTY-TWO

At the armory, Cassie explained the plan and assigned teams. Each team had a driver with some ATV experience. Everyone was happy to learn there would be no long-distance hiking required. She briefed the group on their assigned search areas and explained that the noise of the ATVs would mean that if they spotted one of the birds it would be on the move, so coordination between teams would be key. She passed around pictures of the nest while explaining the main objective for the day was to identify where the Thunderbirds were nesting. Each team had been assigned areas that met the requirement for a nesting site. The trucks and Humvees headed out to the two staging areas Cassie identified, one on the north end of the birds known territory and one on the south end. Though Cassie would have liked to pair up with Hank, she assigned him to a team on the north side and herself to a team on the south.

The search seemed less tedious with the ATVs because you could cover large areas more quickly. Whenever they came to a promising area, they'd leave the ATVs and walk looking for the nest. Each time they stopped, Cassie referred back to the picture to glean every possible clue from it. Just before noon one of the southern teams radioed they had found a nest. They gave coordinates and Cassie drove her ATV to the location. In the meantime, the other teams continued searching. They were hoping to find at least two nesting sites.

Once Cassie saw it, she knew it was a Thunderbird nest. She logged the GPS coordinates and took photographs. One of the soldiers kept watch while Cassie and the other two men did a brief search of the nest. She hoped they could get a sense of how recently it had been used. She knew they might find evidence of other victims in the form of bones, or fabric, or even more body parts. They did find a few scraps of fabric which they bagged and tagged to turn over to the police as well as some bones. No one in the group felt confident in saying whether the bones were human or not. The lab would make that determination.

The team that found the nest stayed in the area watching for the bird until time to return to the staging area for the night. Cassie wanted to continue searching. There should be at least one more nest to find. Tomorrow's search would be focused around the nest they had located. Shortly after the teams had been reminded to check their locations and head back to the staging area to assure they arrived back by 6:00 PM, one of the northern teams radioed they had found something. Hank was nearer than Cassie, so he went to investigate. The radio squawked to life again a few minute later with the report that it was another nest.

On the way back to the armory, Cassie stopped to deliver all the evidence gathered to the police station for analysis. The BITES team had dinner together and everyone seemed pleased with how the search was going. Cassie filled them in on the plan for the coming day which would likely be the last day the military teams would participate regardless of the outcome. The group would be divided between the two nest sites and would use the ATVs to search an expanding ring out from each nest. This should provide a good likelihood they would find the bird.

Jim had been very quiet and hadn't made any comments about Cassie's planning of the operation. She'd dealt with people like Jim before. If the operation was successful, Jim would take credit for her work, and if it failed, she would get all the blame. *Sometimes life's just not fair.*

CHAPTER FIFTY-THREE

The string of early mornings and long days showed in the reddened eyes and frequent yawns of the team as they prepared for the day's hunt. They reviewed the objectives and assigned search areas. At the staging locations, every one made sure the ATV tanks were filled and supplies replenished before heading out. They all converged on their assigned nest by the time the sun was fully up. The bird was spotted before noon near the northern nest site. Everyone was ordered to converge on the area as quickly as possible.

Cassie's nerves were on edge as she drove the ATV to the coordinates provided. The ATV's parked well back from the bird and the team started to form a circle around it as they had the last time they cornered one of the birds. They maintained silence as they moved in to surround it. They remained at least fifty yards away. Weapons were aimed and everyone was focused on the target. They had learned from their previous experience that tightening the circle and tranquilizing the bird needed to happen simultaneously. Jim gave the signal, and Cassie fired. Garrett shot next and missed. As Cassie readied her second shot a shadow came over head as the bird flapped its tremendous wings and tried to fly over the hunters. The tranquilizer had a minimal effect, but it made the bird unable to fly. The huge wings flapped against the ground trapping Cassie and several other members of the team. Chaos ensued.

Trapped under the wing, she had no idea what the bird might do next, but she saw an opportunity. She rolled onto her stomach, realizing only when the pain nearly immobilized her that she'd been injured. Once on her stomach, she aimed her weapon at the bird's chest and fired another tranquilizer round.

From her vantage point, she realized she could crawl out from under the wing by moving closer to the bird's feet. She didn't know whether or not it was a good idea, but it was her only option. She stayed on her stomach using her arms to propel her forward. She winced every time she used her left arm, but she made it out and ran away from the bird to get a better shot.

The bird hadn't moved, but it still hadn't fallen. It took a wobbly step back and then another, and then its foot came down on top of Jim, which threw them both off balance. Jim fell, and the Thunderbird stepped on him before it toppled over.

Cassie tried to spot her BITES team in the ensuing chaos. She saw Garrett and Pat helping the wounded, but she couldn't see Hank. Panic started setting in, but then she saw him working with some of the soldiers to secure the fallen bird.

Cassie looked around and saw Jim still on the ground. The bird had stepped right on his chest. He was breathing and conscious though it was clear that he had internal injuries from the weight of the mammoth creature. She called for a medic. After the medic took care of Jim, he checked out Cassie's shoulder. He stabilized it as well as possible. When she got to the hospital, they'd put it back in place. It would be fine after a few days, but she'd need some serious pain meds if she wanted to be comfortable.

Hank, Cassie, and a few of the uninjured soldiers remained with the bird until the helicopter arrived to remove it. The medevac chopper had already transported Jim to the hospital. When the chopper arrived to load the bird, Cassie watched the operation with a tinge of sadness. She knew it couldn't end any other way, but she still felt the loss of these magnificent creatures that they had only started to get to know. Cassie didn't have much to say on the ride back to the staging area. She couldn't drive with her immobilized arm, so Hank drove.

X X X

The ER doctor put Cassie's dislocated shoulder back in place and sent her home with Hank and pain medication. She was asleep before they left the hospital parking lot. While Hank waited for Cassie to be released, he'd found Garrett and Pat in the waiting room. Jim was in surgery, and it would be a few hours before they knew the extent of his injuries. Hank told them he was taking Cassie home and would stay with her because of the meds. He asked them to call his cell when they had news about Jim's condition.

Hank stopped at the hotel and checked out of his room. He would be taking care of Cassie for at least the next couple of days. He carried her into the condo and put her into bed. She didn't even stir.

Hank unpacked some of his stuff and set up his PC at the kitchen counter where he could work while keeping an eye on Cassie in case she woke up and needed anything. He prepared his report and submitted it to BITES. He called his military contacts to check on the soldiers who'd been injured. Jim was in the worst shape. Everyone else had fairly minor injuries. Hank found Cassie's phone and called Bob. He filled him in on the op and on Cassie's condition. Bob told Hank he'd drop by later with some food so Hank could concentrate on taking care of Cassie. It was good to know Cassie had a friend like Bob close by.

Hank caught up on email and was brewing some coffee when Cassie moaned. She woke up just enough to ask where she was and why she was so sleepy. Hank explained, and she smiled, closed her eyes, and drifted back to sleep.

Bob stopped by with Cassie's favorite foods--spaghetti and meatballs, Chinese takeout, and the biggest cinnamon roll Hank ever saw. He also brought along groceries he thought they might need like milk, Diet Coke, eggs, and cheese. He checked on Cassie and felt better having seen her for himself. He told Hank to call if they needed anything and to have Cassie give him a call when she was feeling up to it.

Hank wanted to stay close to Cassie in case she needed anything, but worried he might bump her injured shoulder, so he tried sleeping on the sofa but kept waking to check on her. Finally, he eased himself into bed beside her and was able to get a little sleep. In the middle of the night, Cassie woke with a scream of pain. She had turned over onto the bad arm and the pain meds had worn thin by that time. Hank explained what had happened. He helped her take a dose of medication with a glass of water. After talking a few minutes, she faded back into sleep.

Hank had showered and dressed with no sign that Cassie was waking up. He brewed himself a cup of coffee and the aroma woke her. "What's that delicious smell?" she called from the bedroom.

He helped her into a sitting position, and she greedily accepted the steaming mug. She looked at her arm holding the cup and realized she was filthy. After the coffee worked its magic, she struggled through a shower and managed to get dressed. She took a seat at the counter and asked Hank what she had missed. He filled her in, while he cooked breakfast. They spent a quiet day relaxing on the sofa with Cassie drifting off to sleep regularly. By evening, she decided to try forgoing the pain meds for Tylenol. She hated feeling like she was losing time she could never get back. Pat called to let them know that Jim was expected to make a full recovery, but he'd be on medical leave for a while.

CHAPTER FIFTY-FOUR

Hank's departure a few days later was difficult for both of them. They'd gotten used to being together, and neither of them wanted that to change. They tried to talk about where their relationship was going but neither one of them seemed to know what they wanted to say, so for now things would remain as they were. That was the plan they agreed to on their last night together. When they shared a final hug at the airport, Hank whispered in her ear, "I love you, Cassie," and walked through the screening lane before she had time to respond. She had the whole drive back to Las Cruces to worry about what she should have said or would say when he called from Montana later. She had promised herself not to over think this, but she really wasn't good at that.

Over the next few weeks, Cassie spent some time at the shooting range working her shoulder back into competition shape. She checked in with her teammates weekly. Jim was released from the hospital and went to his sister's in Las Vegas to recuperate until he could be home alone. Cassie's fame within BITES was growing. Hank told her how much he missed her every time they spoke. Cassie's condo seemed like something was missing without Hank.

Bob and Cassie had lunch weekly, and he told her how much he liked Hank. One day several weeks later, Bob and Cassie met to go for a hike in the desert. Cassie wanted to go back to area where they first spotted the giant Thunderbird. She scanned the ridge in the distance as she had before and saw nothing. Just as she was turning to go, something caught her eye. She thought she saw something move behind the ridgeline.

"Bob, do you see something behind that next ridge?" Cassie asked.

Bob took her arm and turned her around. "Let's head home, Cassie. You do remember what happened last time you spotted something in the distance don't you?"

ABOUT JO CAREY

Jo Carey grew up in the Midwest but her curiosity and gypsy-spirit has kept her on the move. She's lived in eight US states and spent three years living in Ireland. She has always loved creature movies, so creatures and bugs often show up in her books.

Jo, a former information security compliance guru, writes fast-paced, character-driven stories in a variety of genres from medical thrillers to space operas and cozy mysteries. Her novels are filled with humor, romance, and sometimes creatures or aliens, or maybe even all of the above. She often builds her stories around a strong female lead character surrounded by plenty of hunky male heroes.

Jo's been under fire on a golf course and climbed out the roof of an elevator in the Netherlands. Life hasn't been boring. Now residing in Texas, setting often plays a huge role in her stories. Jo was intrigued by the League of Planetary Systems, a world her husband, Frank, created for his science fiction books, and she now writes mysteries and other types of tales sets in that world. Jo was bitten by a cat, a fire ant, and a snake, before succumbing to the bite of the writing bug.

Jo is currently working on a romance series set in Santa Fe, New Mexico. The four-book series has a story set in each of the four seasons.

Jo hasn't had personal contact with a cryptid or an alien, but it's never too late.

Jo and her husband, Frank, produce a podcast—Xtreme Self-Publishing—which details their self-publishing efforts.

Jo can be reached through the podcast at xtremeselfpublishing.podbean.com or via e-mail at elvenindustriespress@gmail.com or xsppodcast@gmail.com

Jo's Amazon Author page:

http://amazon.com/author/jocarey